The Return of the Plant That Ate Dirty Socks

Other Avon Camelot Books by
Nancy McArthur

THE PLANT THAT ATE DIRTY SOCKS

NANCY MCARTHUR has been writing since her father brought home a typewriter when she was eleven years old. She is the author of two books for younger readers, *Megan Gets a Dollhouse* and *Pickled Peppers,* as well as the Avon Camelot *The Plant That Ate Dirty Socks,* the prequel to this book. In addition to writing, Ms. McArthur teaches journalism at Baldwin-Wallace College, her alma mater. She lives in Berea, Ohio.

The Return of the Plant That Ate Dirty Socks

Nancy McArthur

AN AVON  CAMELOT BOOK

THE RETURN OF THE PLANT THAT ATE DIRTY SOCKS is an original publication of Avon Books. This work has never before appeared in book form. This work is a novel, and while some portions deal with actual locations, this story should in no way be considered factual.

AVON BOOKS
A division of
The Hearst Corporation
105 Madison Avenue
New York, New York 10016

First Avon Camelot Printing: June 1990

CAMELOT TRADEMARK REG. U.S. PAT. OFF. AND IN OTHER COUNTRIES, MARCA REGISTRADA, HECHO EN U.S.A.

Printed in the U.S.A.

OPM   10   9   8   7   6   5   4

This book is dedicated
to all the readers who wanted
the story to continue.
Here is what you asked for.
Have fun reading!

Special thanks to Barbara Berg McArthur, Alison Rolland, Ross Rolland, Karen Rolland, Bill Rolland, Peg Neeson, Fran Hanrahan, and all the teachers and librarians who have been so enthusiastic about *The Plant That Ate Dirty Socks*.

Chapter 1

"Wake up! Something weird is happening!"

Without opening his eyes, Michael mumbled a sleepy reply to his younger brother Norman. "Something weird is always happening since we got our plants. Tell me about it later when it's time to get up."

"No, now!" insisted Norman, who was an expert pest. He bounced on Michael's bed to keep him from going back to sleep.

"Go jump on your own bed," Michael snarled. He tried to kick Norman, but with his feet under the covers he couldn't reach him.

"Get up and look," nagged Norman. "Stanley did something weirder than usual during the night!"

Grumbling, Michael untangled himself from the covers and sat up. Stanley was his very large, very strange plant. Late every night it ate dirty socks. It picked them up with a vine, sucked them into one of its ice-cream-cone–shaped leaves, and later burped.

Norman's plant, named Fluffy, was a little smaller

1

and ate only clean socks. Fluffy also burped and then made a noise that sounded like "Ex" because Norman had tried to teach his plant to say "Excuse me."

Michael rubbed his eyes. Stanley did look different.

"See?" said Norman. "He grew little green thingies all over." He handed Michael the magnifying glass from his detective kit.

There were hundreds of them. "These look like seed pods!" said Michael. "And they're shaped like teeny socks. What about Fluffy?"

"No thingies," Norman replied, sounding disappointed.

"Not yet," said Michael. "Fluffy grows slower and isn't as big yet. He'll probably get pods later."

"Yay!" said Norman.

"No yay," Michael said. "Wait till Mom and Dad see these."

"Uh-oh," said Norman.

"Right. We can't let this wreck our trip to Florida. We need a new master plan."

Just last night Michael had talked Mom and Dad into renting a camper so they could take Stanley and Fluffy along on their three-week vacation. They couldn't leave the plants home in someone else's care without the sock-eating secret leaking. For a while they weren't going to get a vacation because of the plants.

"Mom and Dad will never put up with taking along a plant loaded with seed pods that might fall off from here to Florida," he said.

Norman said hopefully, "Maybe they won't notice."

"These pods are just starting," Michael pointed out. "They'll get big enough to hold the size beans we started these plants with." He plopped back on his pillow.

Last night when he went to sleep, everything was going great, and now this!

"We can pick off all the thingie pods before they get big," said Norman. "If we start right now, maybe we can be done by breakfast. But then we won't have any beans to grow more plants if we want to."

Michael sat up suddenly. "Think what we could do with all these seed pods!"

"Fluffy's, too," added Norman, "when he grows some." He patted Fluffy's vines and leaves.

"Yeah," said Michael, "we'd have enough to start a seed-selling business! People kept saying at the science fair they wished they could grow plants this big, so we could probably sell lots right at school. And what about all those people who saw them on TV and bought pet plants?"

In his imagination he saw packets of seeds going out in the mail and dollar bills coming in, hundreds of them.

"If only we didn't have to keep the sock-eating secret," Norman said. "And if we could grow plants to sell, we'd make more money than with seeds. Millions! We could buy our own pizza place and eat take-out pizza every night!"

Michael nodded. "We could build more rooms on the house. We could each have our own room. That would be great. Or even better, two rooms apiece. I could have a special one for all my stuff."

He was a naturally messy person and liked to save everything. Keeping his stuff picked up and put away was quite a strain, but it was part of the deal with their parents to be allowed to keep the plants.

He pictured a room where he could spread out all his

3

junk and drop things on the floor wherever he felt like it. He could be as messy as he wanted in there and still keep his bedroom clean so his plant couldn't eat anything but the dirty socks it needed to stay healthy. Then he could hire somebody to come in once a year to clean up the messy room. Or maybe just every two years.

"Plants would be harder to mail than seeds," he said, "but maybe we could figure out how. We could be famous for our plant-eating socks."

"Huh?" said Norman.

"I mean sock-eating plants. I'm not completely awake yet. We'd be helping kids all over the world keep their rooms clean. Maybe we could sell them to mothers, too. They're the ones who always want rooms clean. I'll bet mothers would pay a lot."

"So would kids who have to share rooms with messy brothers," said Norman.

"And sisters," Michael continued, ignoring Norman's dig. "I could do great commercials." He picked up his hairbrush for a microphone. "Do you have a messy room? Is your mother driving you crazy with all the yelling to clean up? Are you up to your belly button in junk? Get a handy-dandy lovable monster plant. It'll force you to keep your room clean and like it!"

"I want to do the commercials, too," whined Norman.

"Maybe we could take turns once in a while," said Michael. "And here's our company's expert neatness nut to tell you about his plant-eating pet sock—pet-eating sock plant—whatever!" He handed over the hairbrush.

Norman jumped up on his own bed and sang loudly

into the hairbrush: "Buy a pet plant to keep your room clean. Then your brother can't mess up the room anymore, doo-dah, doo-dah!"

"What kind of commercial is that?" exclaimed Michael, rolling his eyes.

"A music video," Norman said, adding a few moves he apparently thought were dance steps.

"That's terrible!"

"I don't care," sang Norman. "Buy seeds and plants and send us lots of money, doo-dah, doo-dah!" He went on and on. Michael put his pillow around his ears to muffle the noise.

The door opened. Mom, blinking sleepily, asked, "Are you two all right? I heard howling."

"Singing!" said Norman indignantly.

"Of course, singing," said Mom. "I should have guessed. You'll have to shut up or at least do it quietly. You woke me up, but your father's still asleep."

"Quiet singing is no fun," Norman said, pouting.

"Then wait half an hour until it's time to get up," Mom said, and closed the door.

"She didn't see the thingies," whispered Norman.

"Maybe they're too small to see from the door," said Michael. He tiptoed over there to check. "No, you can't see them from here. They're as green as the leaves, so they blend in. We probably have a few days until they get bigger to figure out what to do."

Norman got busy getting dressed. Then he watered Fluffy with his Super Splasher Water Blaster, a much bigger than usual water pistol. He wheeled his plant around to get sun on the other side. Both plants were securely fastened to skateboards for easy moving.

Michael tried to go back to sleep, but thoughts of making tons of money in the seeds and plants business kept him awake until the alarm clock rang.

If only there were some way to persuade Mom and Dad to let them out of the promise to keep the plants' sock-eating a secret. How could you sell sock-eating plants without telling people that they ate socks?

Chapter 2

At breakfast Mom and Dad were talking excitedly about vacation plans.

"It'll be a three-day drive," Dad said.

"After the first night at a campground," said Mom, "we can spend the next night at my mother's because that's only a hundred miles out of the way. The third night we'll be in Florida at the campground where we'll spend our vacation."

Dad said, "I'll make some calls today to find out where we can rent a camper. What do you think about getting one of those really deluxe ones, like a motel room on wheels?"

"Yes," Mom said. "We haven't had a real vacation in two years. We've been saving up, so let's go first-class. Let's get five-day tickets for Disney World. After that we can go to some of the other attractions around there."

The boys sat there making crunching noises with their cereal.

"You guys are awfully quiet," Dad said. "Aren't you excited about the trip?"

"Yes!" said Michael. "I'm just sitting here thinking about it."

"Me, too," sang Norman. "I can hardly wait to tell Bob and everybody else at school. Doo-dah, doo-dah!"

"Why are you singing?" asked Dad. "That is singing, isn't it?"

Norman glared at him, but he had just taken a big bite of cereal and his mouth was too full to say anything.

Michael changed the subject. "Is it OK to tell people we're taking the plants along?"

"Why not?" said Mom. "Everybody in town already saw them either at the science fair or on TV. People already think we're a little strange because we have these weird plants. So taking them on vacation won't seem all that odd. Not for this family. Just don't tell anybody why we can't leave them home with a plant-sitter."

"OK, OK, OK," sang Norman, wiggling across the kitchen to put his cereal bowl in the sink.

"What on earth is he doing?" asked Dad, astonished.

"He's dancing," Michael said, "but don't ask why."

Michael put his dish in the sink. Gathering up his school things, he hurried out of the house. He wanted to get going way ahead of Norman. In case the kid decided to sing or dance on the way to school, he didn't want to be seen with him.

By the time Michael got to school he was still thinking about what he could buy with tons of money. In the crowded hall he was startled out of his daydream by Jason, the only person outside his family who knew the plants ate socks. He found out by accident at a sleepover when he woke up in the middle of the night in time to see Stanley eating dinner.

Jason asked, "How did things go last night? You were supposed to call me. And what did the principal want to talk to you about after school?"

"Mr. Leedy wants to have a Pet Plant Day next fall starring Stanley and Fluffy. Mom and Dad agreed we can keep them until then. So they're saved for a few months. After that I'll have to think of a new master plan."

"What about all the junk we put in your room to show your folks what it would look like if they made you get rid of your plants?"

"It was a disaster."

Jason laughed. "Your mom must have been really mad when she saw all that junk!"

"It's easy for you to laugh. You didn't hang around to help clean up!"

"I had to leave. My mom was picking me up."

"Sure," said Michael.

"Really," Jason said. "And it all turned out OK, didn't it? You get to keep Stanley and Fluffy."

"Yeah, and next month we're going to Florida on vacation."

"Lucky you! I'll feed your plants. I can take them over to my house. Or I can get my mom to drive me over every night to put out the socks. I won't tell her what they're eating, just that they need watering every night."

"No, thanks," said Michael. "We're taking them along."

"You're taking what along where?" asked his friend Chad, coming up to join them.

"My family's going to Florida next month."

9

"Great! When I was there, I didn't want to come home. Can I take care of your plants while you're gone?"

"Thanks, but we're taking them along."

"To take them on a plane, you'll have to buy them their own seats," joked Chad.

"We're renting a camper and driving."

Chad chuckled. "You'd better rent the biggest one there is," he said.

By the end of lunch period, the vacation news was all over the building, and sixteen more kids had asked Michael if he needed a plant-sitter.

In the principal's office Mr. Leedy was breaking the news about Pet Plant Day to the custodian. Mr. Jones had been very suspicious of the night noises and other strange happenings near the plants during the science fair.

"You're going to bring those weird monster plants back into this building? On purpose?" asked Mr. Jones. "Maybe you haven't thought this through carefully. There haven't been any haunted noises in the gym since the science fair ended and those things went home. You didn't hear all those schlurps and burps from that corner at night. It would chill your blood! Mark my words. Those plants are not normal!"

"Those plants are famous," said Mr. Leedy, "and this pet plant idea has got all the children really excited about growing things. So we're going to make a learning experience out of it. Here's a picture of the platform we need you to build for Fluffy and Stanley. We'll need spotlights for them, too."

Mr. Jones looked over the drawing. "A cage would be better," he said.

10

"What have you got against plants?" asked Mr. Leedy. "I've had this spider plant in my office for years and take it home every summer. And I noticed you have a couple of little ones on the windowsill in your toolroom."

"Sure, but I don't give them dingdong names like Jerry Geranium and Woof-Woof, the way the kids are doing since this pet plant thing got started."

Chapter 3

Every day the pods grew bigger.

"We'd better tell them," Michael announced. "They'll be a lot madder if they notice the pods on their own."

"You tell them," said Norman. "It's your plant."

The boys had to make their own beds and clean their room, so their parents seldom came in any farther than the doorway during the day. They usually came all the way in to say good night and make the boys turn the lights out. So far, they had not noticed the pods.

"Until I figure out how to tell them," said Michael, "let's get in bed and turn out the lights before they come in to say good night. They can't see the pods in the dark."

The first night they did this Mom remarked, "This is a nice change. We didn't have to tell you two or three times to get into bed and turn out the lights. You guys must be really tired."

The second night she wondered if they were getting sick. She felt their foreheads and asked a lot of questions.

After Mom and Dad said good night in the dark and

went in the living room to watch TV, Mom said, "They're not sick, so they must be up to something."

They went back to the boys' room, turned on the lights, and stood in the doorway looking around. Everything seemed the same as usual.

"Please turn those lights off," said Michael. "We're trying to sleep in here!"

"Yeah," said Norman, quickly stuffing under the covers a comic book and the flashlight he had been reading it with.

Mom sat down on Michael's bed. "Why are the lights already out when we come in here to say good night? Is there something you don't want us to notice?"

"I was going to tell you in the morning," Michael replied. "As soon as I figured out how to tell you so you won't get mad."

"You know you can tell us anything," said Mom soothingly. "I'll even promise not to get mad. What is it?"

"Seed pods," said Michael. "On Stanley." Mom turned to look.

"Oh, no!" she exclaimed, looking horrified. "Hundreds of them!"

Dad looked closely at Stanley. Then he inspected Fluffy. "Nothing on this one, thank goodness," he said.

"Not yet," said Norman, "but pretty soon, I hope."

"Let's all try to stay calm," said Mom, pacing back and forth.

"We already are calm," Michael pointed out. "Except you."

Mom took a deep breath. "I promised not to get mad," she reminded herself. "That was a dumb promise." She took another deep breath. "We're not going to let this ruin our vacation.'' She gave Stanley a dirty look. ''Nothing is going to stop us.''

''Right,'' said Michael. ''Before we go, we're going to pick all the pods off. And if Fluffy gets pods, we'll pick those, too. So seeds won't fall off all the way from here to Florida. Nothing to worry about.''

Mom glared at Dad. ''Aren't you upset about this?'' she asked.

''No,'' said Dad. ''After the seeds are all picked off, we can burn them in the fireplace. No problem.''

''No!'' argued Michael. ''We could make a bunch of money selling them. People would pay a lot for seeds to grow plants that force kids to keep their rooms clean.''

''He's got a point,'' Dad told Mom, ''but unfortunately we can't tell anybody that they eat socks. If we could find some way to sell them without anyone knowing that they came from us . . .''

Mom shouted at Dad, ''You're not actually considering such a wacko idea!''

''Not seriously,'' said Dad. ''Just thinking about the possibilities.''

Michael suggested quickly, ''We don't have to argue about this right now. We can argue after we get back from vacation.''

Mom took another deep breath. ''Stay calm,'' she said to herself. ''Very calm.''

In the morning Mom laid down the law. ''Nobody goes in your room except the four of us. Nobody sees those seeds.''

''Not even Bob?'' Norman asked about his best friend.

''No,'' said Dad, ''and not Jason, either.''

''Yeah,'' said Norman. ''He tried to blackmail me to get my plant.''

14

"Not exactly," said Michael. "He just said he wouldn't tell about the plants eating socks if you gave him yours. He probably figured it was worth a try. But it didn't work. We got him to promise not to tell anyway."

"He really wanted Fluffy," Norman said.

"Well, he's not going to get him," said Michael.

He tried to think of excuses to keep Jason from coming over. It was a good thing he lived far enough away on the other side of town so he couldn't just walk over any time he felt like it. When Jason had arranged for his uncle to drive the plants to the science fair in a limo, he'd sneakily sort of gotten Michael to promise him some seeds even though Michael had been sure there weren't going to be any.

Now there were hundreds of seeds, and he had to make sure Jason did not find out.

But of course Jason wanted to come over. "Let's have another sleep over at your house," he said. "That was fun."

"Not right now," replied Michael. "We're all busy packing for our vacation."

"But you're not going right away."

"It takes us a really long time to pack. We're taking a three-week supply of everything except furniture."

"Then I'll just get my mom to drive me over for Sunday afternoon."

"No, I'd rather come over to your house. I'll get my dad to bring me over Sunday."

"OK," Jason said, but Michael thought he looked a little suspicious.

Chapter 4

Saturday the whole family went to Johnson's Recreational Vehicle Sales and Rental.

Mr. Johnson, who showed them around, explained that hardly anybody called them campers anymore. "They're recreational vehicles, RVs," he said.

There were big tents that folded down into small trailers to tow with cars. There were small trucks with sleeping quarters on the back. Dad stopped at one that looked like a bus.

"Let's look inside this one," he said.

"Where's the doors?" asked Norman.

"Follow me," said Mr. Johnson. He led them around the front to the middle of the other side, where the door was.

The front of the RV was almost flat, with no hood that stuck out. Michael stepped up on the bumper and pressed his hands and face against the huge windshield to peer inside.

"This looks great!" he exclaimed.

"Get off the bumper," said Dad.

Through the side door they stepped up into the RV.

16

"This is wonderful," Mom said.

In the front, a step down, were two big padded seats, one of which was for the driver. Above them under the roof was a sleeping bunk.

In the middle was a living room area. On one side was a couch for sitting in the daytime and sleeping at night. On the other side were padded seats facing a table. Mr. Johnson showed them how the table folded down to form a bed with the seats.

The kitchen part had a small sink, stove, and refrigerator with a microwave oven in the wall.

"Here's a teeny bathroom!" said Norman. They all peeked in around him. A toilet, sink, and shower fitted snugly into a space the size of Michael and Norman's bedroom closet.

Past the bathroom, the whole back of the RV was a little bedroom with just enough room for a double bed.

"This is so nice," said Mom, "I guess I wouldn't mind all four of us being cooped up in here for three weeks."

"All six of us," Michael reminded her.

"You're taking two more people along?" asked Mr. Johnson. "Plenty of room to sleep six."

"Not people," said Mom. "We have to take along two very tall objects that need to stick out of the sunroof." She looked up at the ceiling. "Uh-oh," she said, poking Dad in the ribs. There wasn't any sunroof.

"These RVs are air-conditioned," explained Mr. Johnson. "Sunroofs are a thing of the past. But if you want fresh air circulating, you can open those air vents." He pointed up at two small square vents that had screens over them with fans attached.

Dad whispered to Michael, "Could the tops of you-know-who fit through those?"

"I think so," Michael whispered back. "Their tops are the skinniest parts."

Dad asked Mr. Johnson, "Could you take the screens and fans off so things can stick out?"

"I suppose so," he replied. "But couldn't you just lay them down on the floor?"

"No, they really have to stand up and stick out."

"What are these," joked Mr. Johnson, "baby giraffes?"

"Actually," said Dad, "they're very tall plants."

"You're taking giant plants on your vacation?"

"It's too complicated to explain," explained Dad.

"Wait a minute," said Mr. Johnson. "Are you by any chance the family with the big pet plants? I read about them in the paper."

"We were on TV, too," said Norman.

"You must love those plants," said Mr. Johnson. "Taking anything that big along in an RV would be a real pain in the neck."

Mom explained, "These plants need special care. We can't go off and leave them with somebody else."

"So, do you think you could fix the holes in the roof for them?" Dad asked.

"I'm sure we can work it out," said Mr. Johnson. "Of course, the plants will have to wear seat belts."

"But they can't sit down," said Norman.

"I don't mean sitting-down seat belts," said Mr. Johnson. "I mean strapping them in one place so they can't fall over or fly through the air and hit you when you make a sharp turn or a sudden stop. You can't have anything lying around loose in a moving RV."

"Do they have to wear seat belts at night?" asked Norman.

"Only when you're driving," said Mr. Johnson.

"I'm not old enough to drive yet," said Norman, glaring up at him as if he ought to know that.

"Then why don't you go sit in the driver's seat and pretend you're practicing," he said. "Just don't touch anything."

Norman stopped to peer up into the bunk over the front seats. "Boost me up," he asked Dad. He crawled into the bunk. "This is my bed." he said.

"We'll see," said Mom.

"One other thing about your plants," said Mr. Johnson. "With the tops sticking out they would take quite a beating from the wind force of driving. The leaves would get badly shredded, I think, unless you figured out a way to cover them securely."

"We can do that," said Dad.

"And you'd better put some plastic sheeting under them to protect the carpet."

"Fine," Dad said.

"Then you're all set," said Mr. Johnson, "for a wonderful, relaxing vacation you'll never forget."

The next Saturday morning Mom and Dad went to practice RV driving in Johnson's parking lot. Norman was down the street at Bob's. Michael was home alone picking pods off Stanley. He was daydreaming about being a seed-business millionaire when the front doorbell rang.

He thought maybe Norman had locked himself out, but the door was not locked. When he opened it, there, leaning on a bike, stood Jason.

"Look what I got for my birthday," said Jason. "Now I can ride over here any time I want. I don't have to wait for when my mom can drive me."

Michael did not know what to do. He certainly couldn't

invite him in. He looked the bike over. "This is great," he said.

"Want to try it?" asked Jason. "Take it for a ride around the block." Of course Michael wanted to try it. And going around the block would give him a few minutes to figure out what to do.

"Wait for me right here in the yard," he said. "OK?"

"Sure," Jason replied.

"Don't move," added Michael. "I'll be right back." He pushed off, pedaling slowly at first to get the feel of the bike, then faster. It glided so smoothly that it felt like sailing along the street. A dog ran along, barking, and then gave up. Michael waved at neighbors as he sped by.

Rounding the last corner, he could see his front yard not far off. Jason wasn't there!

Chapter 5

Michael screeched to a stop on his front walk and dropped the bike on the grass. "Jason!" he yelled, hoping to hear an answering shout from the backyard. There was no reply.

Just as he reached for the handle of the front door, it opened. Out came Jason.

"What are you doing?" asked Michael. "You were supposed to wait for me out here."

"I needed to use your bathroom."

"Oh," replied Michael, trying to sound casual. He didn't want to ask Jason if he had looked at the plants. If he hadn't, the question would make him suspicious. Besides, Michael thought with relief, if he had seen them, he'd be all excited and asking for seeds.

"Gotta go," Jason said.

"It's a great bike," said Michael.

Jason rode off with a wave.

Michael went back in to finish pod-picking. By the time he got them all off Stanley, they almost filled a pail.

When Norman got home, he told him about the close

call with Jason. "But now that all the pods are picked off," he said, "we can let Jason or Bob or anybody in, and nobody will know."

Norman was dusting Fluffy's leaves carefully with a washcloth. He stopped to pick up his magnifying glass. "No, we can't," he replied. "Look. Now Fluffy's starting to have babies!"

Michael looked. Tiny sock-shaped seed pods were sprouting all over Fluffy. Norman said, "Will they be big enough to pick off before we go to Florida?"

"I hope so," replied Michael.

Norman looked up and down Fluffy. "My plant has more pods than your plant," he boasted.

Michael did not want to get into a pod-counting contest with Norman because it would take too long.

"We'll see," he said. "One thing for sure is that we'll have two pails full of pods."

Mom and Dad gave the boys safety instructions about riding in an RV. Mom talked to their teachers and Mr. Leedy about how this was the only time they could take their vacation. She got them excused from school for an extra ten days after spring vacation as long as they did homework on the trip.

Dad went to the Save-A-Lot discount store, which had the cheapest socks prices. He bought a three-week supply of socks for the plants' vacation meals. He got plenty of white ones with brown stripes. Norman called these fudge ripple, which he believed was Fluffy's favorite flavor.

Dad also bought big sheets of plastic to put on the RV floor and to wrap the tops of the plants.

Meanwhile, Norman started picking Fluffy's pods as soon as they were big enough.

The night before their trip, Dad drove the RV home and backed it into the driveway. It took up the whole drive.

The family started carrying things out and stowing them in the storage cupboards. Bob came over to help.

When no one else was looking, Bob and Norman smuggled in Norman's Water Blaster and rubber gorilla head. They tucked them under the mattress up in Norman's bunk.

Some neighbors came over to see the RV. Norman and Bob gave them guided tours.

Michael unrolled the plastic through the kitchen and living room areas, where the plants would stand under the air vents. Dad used masking tape to hold it firmly in place.

Now they were ready to load the plants, so they wouldn't have to take time to do it in the morning. They rolled Stanley out the front door and carefully hoisted him up the narrow steps into the RV.

Michael scrambled up the outside ladder to the roof and gently guided Stanley's top through the opening.

"OK?" he called down the hole.

"Fine," said Dad. "Stanley takes up more space than I thought, but we can work around him."

Michael climbed down to see. The cooking area seemed full of leaves and vines, like having a tree in the kitchen.

Mom stared at what little space was left for fixing meals. She did not look pleased. "Don't be surprised if you find a few leaves in your lunch," she said.

They hauled Fluffy in and settled him in the living room area.

"We'll strap them in and wrap their tops in the morning," said Dad. "That won't take long. We roll at dawn!"

"Let's sit down and try to get used to this space," Mom said, brushing leaves away from her face.

Norman sat in the driver's seat, twisting the steering wheel and saying, "Zoooooooom."

"Stop that," said Dad.

Norman paid no attention. He was having too much fun pretending to be driving. He twisted a few knobs on the dashboard. Nothing happened. He twisted another one. The huge windshield wipers rose up and went *Thwump-thwump, thwump-thwump*.

Dad reached over Norman and twisted some knobs until he found the right one. The wipers thwumped down and stayed there.

"Don't touch anything," Dad warned, "or else."

Norman said, "If Fluffy's sleeping out here tonight, I want to, too. He'll be lonesome without me."

"You can't stay out here alone," Dad said. "And I want to get a good night's sleep in my own bed before we start this trip."

Michael thought it might be fun to sleep in the driveway. He could take the back bedroom. That would be almost as good as having his own room. "I could stay out here, too," he said. "We can lock the door."

"Well," said Dad, "if it's all right with your mother."

"I suppose it would be OK," Mom said. "But no fighting or horsing around."

The boys got ready for bed in the house. Mom and Dad came out with them to tuck them in. Dad gave Norman a boost up to the back of the driver's seat. He scrambled up into the bunk from there. Michael put the plants' socks meal within easy reach.

He stretched out in the big bed, enjoying being far from Norman. But after a while, he called, "Are you still awake?" There was no reply.

24

Michael was so excited about leaving early in the morning that he thought he would never fall asleep. But he drifted off soon after Norman did.

Later, in the silence, Fluffy and Stanley began reaching around in the dark of this unfamiliar place. They found their socks, ate, and burped. Then their vines felt around as far as they could reach.

Fluffy was close enough to reach up into the bunk. He found Norman there and touched him lightly on the head. Then he withdrew his vine and settled down.

In the middle of the night, Norman woke up. He had to go to the bathroom. Groggily he got out of bed. Much to his surprise, the floor wasn't there!

He landed standing backward in the driver's seat. Not knowing where he was, he backed right into the horn.

Still mostly asleep, he wondered where that loud noise was coming from. It went on and on.

Michael was so deeply asleep that the horn did not wake him up at first. He was dreaming about Disney World. The parade he was watching suddenly had some cars in it with horns blowing.

Soon Dad and Mom, awakened by the noise, were outside pounding on the locked RV door. When the boys did not come immediately, Mom ran back in the house to find the keys.

Dad stepped up on the bumper and pressed his hands and face against the windshield to look in.

Norman turned and saw a squashed face staring at him with two big hands reaching out to clutch him. He screamed and hit the windshield wiper knob. The huge wipers rose and—THWUMP!—wiped Dad right off the windshield.

Dad suffered only scraped knuckles in his plunge off the bumper. He made the boys come back in the house to finish the night in their own beds. It took a long time for everyone to fall asleep again.

So they did not roll at dawn. Mom and Dad slept through their alarm, woke up about 10 A.M., and awakened the boys.

They all hurried to put the last few things into the RV. They took one last look around the house to make sure they had everything. When Michael went up on the RV roof to put the plastic over the plants' tops, he noticed a couple of seed pods still on Fluffy. He pulled them off and put them in his pocket. Mom checked her checklist and locked up the house. "Let's roll!" she said.

As they piled into the RV, Norman asked, "What about breakfast?"

"We'll eat on the way," Dad said. "We have to get going."

"I'm hungry now," whined Norman.

"Me, too," Michael said.

Mom said, "We'll eat while your father drives, and then I'll drive for a while so he can eat."

"I thought you were going to drive first," said Dad, a little crossly.

"That was when we were rolling at dawn," Mom snapped. "It's time for you to take over the wheel."

"But we haven't driven anywhere yet," Dad complained, "and I'm hungry right now!"

"No fair," said Mom. "I want to eat now!"

Michael shook his head. This was going to be some trip if his parents were acting like this before they even got out of the driveway. "You sound just like me and Norman," he remarked. That stopped them.

"All right," said Mom. "We'll all eat right now. It'll

be easier when we're not moving." She squeezed past Stanley and handed out the bowls, spoons, glasses, bananas, cereal, orange juice, and milk.

Someone rapped on the window next to the table. It was Mrs. Smith from down the street. "What a clever idea!" she called to them. "Camping out in your own driveway! This certainly will save a lot of money on gas and campground fees!"

They invited her in. She elbowed her way past Fluffy so she could sit down. She brushed leaves away from in front of her face so she could talk without getting them in her mouth.

"You're camping out with your plants?" she asked. "Wouldn't it be easier just to run in the house to water them?"

Dad explained, "They're going with us on vacation. We're leaving for Florida as soon as we finish eating."

"We roll at noon," said Michael, doubling over with laughter.

They finally rolled a little before noon. Mrs. Smith waved good-bye in the front yard. The huge vehicle lurched slowly out of the driveway and down the street, with Dad at the wheel, Mom and the boys waving out the windows, and the two weird plants sticking up out of the air vents.

Chapter 6

The boys found out right away that riding in an RV was not like riding in a car. Even though they sat on a chair or a couch, they had to wear seat belts. Mom made them start their homework, but when they turned a sharp corner, the books and papers slid right off the table.

"When we eat pizza," said Norman, "we're going to have to glue the box down first."

Michael unbuckled for a minute to get a snack from the refrigerator. While he was standing in front of it with the door open, Dad, about to make another turn, warned, "Hang on!" Michael did, but pop cans and apples fell out and rolled around the floor.

"Just close the door," Mom said with a sigh. "We'll catch them when we stop."

Later, turning into a gas station caught Norman off balance. He plopped backward into a plastic wastebasket and got stuck. It took Dad pulling on the wastebasket and Mom and Michael pulling on Norman to free him.

Afterward Michael laughed and called him "wastebasket butt." That started a big fight.

Mom made Michael sit up front with Dad. She took Norman into the back bedroom and read to him for a while.

After starting so much later than planned, they were not going to get as far as the campground where they had a reservation. On another gas stop, Mom called to cancel the reservation. She started looking in a directory for another campground they could get to that night.

They drove well past sundown to make up for lost time. Mom made the boys change into their pajamas and brush their teeth. They put socks out for the plants. Lulled by the motion of driving along the highway, the boys fell asleep.

They woke up when they felt the RV slow to a stop.

"Are we at the campground?" asked Norman sleepily.

"Not exactly," Dad said.

Michael looked out the window. Instead of the woods and darkness he expected, he saw bright lights and concrete.

They were parked in the vast empty lot of a shopping center with all the stores closed.

"Why are we camping in a shopping center?" he asked.

"We're too tired to drive any farther," Dad explained. "This is the only place we could find to park. Just go back to bed. We'll set the alarm so we can leave here long before the stores open."

But before the alarm went off, they were awakened by a police officer pounding on the door. "You can't park here," he said. "Didn't you see the signs? No overnight parking."

Dad explained why they were there.

"I can sympathize with you," said the officer, "but I

still have to give you a ticket. And you'll have to leave the lot right now. You can mail the fine to the county courthouse.''

Before Mom or Dad could reply, one of the plants gave a very loud burp.

The policeman looked startled, but he just handed Dad the ticket. He suggested, ''If you get back on the interstate, there's a rest area where you can park about fifteen miles from here.''

Only a few RVs were on the road that early. Theirs was the only one driven by a woman wearing pink pajamas.

When they got to the rest area, Mom parked, pulled down the shades, and announced, ''We're taking a nap!''

''I'm hungry,'' Norman whined.

Mom tossed him a box of cereal. ''Have a couple of handfuls,'' she said. ''We'll do breakfast later.'' She went in the back bedroom and went to sleep.

Norman, the only one awake, munched some cereal and watered Fluffy with his Blaster. He was still hungry, so he made himself a grape jelly and lettuce sandwich.

Michael was sleeping with his mouth open. Norman thought about squirting water into it with his Blaster. He decided not to, but he enjoyed thinking about it.

When they got going later in the morning, Dad explained that if they had got to the campground as planned last night, today would have been a short drive to Grandma's. But now it would be just a little longer drive.

The boys were too tired to fight, so it was a fairly quiet day.

After Norman drove everybody crazy by reading every road sign out loud, they finally pulled into Grandma's driveway with the horn honking.

Grandma, in jeans and sweatshirt, was digging in a flower bed in her front yard. She hurried over to give them all hugs and kisses as they came out the RV door.

"We brought our plants along," Norman said, pointing to the roof. Grandma looked up. "They're bigger than I thought," she remarked.

"They grew since we sent you the picture," said Norman.

Grandma stepped up into the RV. "This is wonderful," she said. "It looks like it has everything."

"Yes, " Mom said, "but we'll be glad to sleep in a house tonight!"

"Are you having a good time on your vacation?" asked Grandma.

"Not so far," Dad replied.

"Which one is Fluffy?" Grandma asked Norman.

He showed her. "Fluffy," he said, "this is Grandma."

She laughed. "You take after me. I talk to my plants, too. Hello, Fluffy, you certainly are a big one." She turned to Stanley. "This must be yours, Michael."

"Mine's bigger," bragged Michael.

"You both did a wonderful job of growing these," she said. "They look very healthy." She looked a little closer. "I know a lot about plants, but I've never seen anything like these. What are they?"

"We're not sure," said Michael.

"I'll look in some of my plant books later," said Grandma. She broke a little stalk of leaves off Stanley and stuck it in her pocket. "Let's carry your things in the house. Dinner's almost ready."

After dinner Norman wanted to bring the plants in, but Grandma said she'd rather have them stay in the RV.

"Why?" asked Norman, pouting a little.

"I'd rather not have them inside with my house plants. Sometimes plants have diseases or insects that spread to other plants. I know yours probably don't have those things, but I don't want to take a chance. Besides, getting them out of the RV can't be easy. When you leave tomorrow you'd have to lug them back in. That's too much trouble for just one night."

Michael was so tired he sat down on the bed upstairs and put his head down on the pillow just for a minute. Norman fell asleep on the living room couch. Dad carried him upstairs to bed. He decided not to wake the boys to make them change into pajamas. He just pulled off their shoes and covered them with blankets.

Mom and Dad were so tired that they went to bed without realizing that the boys had fallen asleep before going out to the RV to feed the plants.

Grandma sat up a little later, looking through her plant books. She found nothing that matched Stanley's leaves, which she had stuck in a glass of water. Then she went to bed, too.

Later, Stanley's and Fluffy's vines began feeling around for their meals and didn't find them. The vines started creeping all over the RV, as far as they could reach. No Norman. No Michael. No socks.

Norman woke up early as usual. He couldn't think of anything to bother Michael about, so he looked out the window. The RV was gone!

Chapter 7

Norman howled the news into Michael's ear. Michael bounced out of bed and looked out the window to make sure.

"Maybe Dad put it in the garage for the night," Norman said hopefully.

"It's too big for the garage. Besides, Grandma's car was already in there."

Michael suddenly remembered how he fell asleep. "Did you feed the plants?" he asked.

"No," said Norman. "I fell asleep on the couch and woke up here. Didn't you feed them?"

"Uh-oh," said Michael.

"Maybe they drove to a sock store," Norman suggested. "If Fluffy's driving, they won't be gone long."

They woke everyone else up.

Mom and Dad were really upset. Grandma called the police to report that the RV was stolen.

Michael felt terrible. He certainly didn't mind having his homework stolen, and they could buy more clothes and things, but even though they had seeds back home, no new plants could ever replace Stanley or Fluffy.

Grandma said, "Don't worry. I'm sure the police will find the RV, and the plants will probably still be safe inside. They're too big to steal."

Two hours later the police called to say the RV was found. "The giant plants you described are still in it," said the officer on the phone.

They piled into Grandma's car to go to the police station.

"We towed it in because the lock was broken," said the officer at the desk.

"How did you find it?" asked Grandma.

"Some witnesses called in. They heard yelling and saw two guys jumping out of the side door of an RV. They ran off, but the weirdest part was their feet. Each of them had one sock on and one bare foot."

"How strange," Grandma said.

"And in the RV," said the officer, "we found their shoes, but no socks."

"What on earth do you suppose happened in there?" asked Grandma.

After Dad signed some papers and paid the towing charge, they went out the back of the station to get the RV.

Inside, the plants stood in the middle of a mess. The thieves had dumped everything out of the cupboards to look for things worth stealing. They had also stopped for pizza. Two slices sat on the table with one bite out of each one. Two colas were spilled. The rest of the pizza slices were flung all over the place.

"Looks like they sat down to eat with their shoes off," said Grandma, "and then something happened to scare them right out of here. I wonder what."

"What matters," Dad said, "is that we got the RV back."

"And the plants are safe," Michael said.

"Fluffy looks a little sick," said Norman. Michael took him aside and whispered, "He ate a sock that somebody was wearing. That would make him sick, because he only eats clean ones."

"He must have been really hungry to do that," said Norman.

"Then maybe now he knows not to try it again," Michael said.

"Plants that big must be valuable," said the police officer. "It's a good thing they weren't stolen."

"No such luck," Mom muttered. She picked a pepperoni slice off the couch and sat down. "Now we have to clean up this disaster area."

Grandma put an arm around her. "It won't take long if we all pitch in," she said soothingly. "You'd better stay with me another day or two and just relax."

"Good," said Michael. "We need a vacation from our vacation."

They stayed at Grandma's three more days. They had great meals, big beds in big rooms, and a lot of fun with Grandma. Even though Fluffy and Stanley could not come inside, Grandma let the boys put them in the garage. Every afternoon they rolled them out in the yard to get some sun.

Grandma introduced the boys to her plants growing in every room of the house, even the bathroom. She told them interesting things about the different kinds.

She kept looking through plant books, but didn't find anything like Stanley's leaves, which still sat in a glass on her desk.

"There's something about the shape of those plants that reminds me a little of the Venus flytrap," she said, "the one that eats insects. Have you ever seen any insects disappearing around Stanley and Fluffy?"

"No," said Michael. "Never insects."

"And then," she continued, "the leaf looks just a little bit like kudzu."

"Kud-who?" asked Norman.

"Kudzu. It was brought to this country from Asia and planted to feed cattle and keep soil from washing away. But it grows several inches a day. It escaped all over the place. It goes right up telephone poles and wires and trees and over fences. People joke that it will grow over anything that sits still."

"I'd like to see that," said Michael.

"Does kudzu do karate chops?" Norman asked. "Like kung fu?"

He and Grandma had a good giggle over that.

The night before they left, Dad said, "Tomorrow night we'll be in Florida at our campground, and the next day, Disney World!"

"I can hardly wait," said Norman.

"I'm glad you could get your campground reservations changed," Grandma said, "so you could stay with me a little longer. I've loved having you here."

"Staying here," Mom said, "has been a wonderful vacation. I wish we had time to stop again on the way home, but we're going to take the shortest route back."

As they packed, Dad said, "We roll at dawn, I hope."

They did leave just when the sky was getting light with beautiful pink and golden streaks as the sun began to appear.

Grandma gave the boys some spending money for souvenirs.

"Thanks," said Norman. "Now I can buy a baby alligator."

"No," said Grandma. "It's against the law to sell them. They're an endangered species, and they're dangerous."

"Then I'll get a fake one," he said. "I can scare my friends with that if they don't get too close."

On the road, as the day wore on, Norman kept asking, "How many more miles?"

Dad told him to read a book.

"I already read them all," replied Norman.

"Get your markers and draw some pictures."

"I don't want to."

"Well, what do you want to do?"

"Sing."

"No," said Mom.

Dad said, "I know what you can do. Count cows."

"Huh?" said Norman.

"When I was a kid," Dad explained, "my brother and I used to count cows on long car trips. John counted the ones on his side of the car, and I counted the ones on my side."

Michael said, "That's dumb. We haven't seen a cow since we left home, and I'm not counting anything with him."

"Then do trucks," said Dad as three big ones passed them in the left lane. "There are plenty of those, although they're all on one side."

Norman liked that idea. "One, two, three," he said.

"You're not going to sit there saying numbers all day!" Michael exclaimed.

"Four," said Norman. "Be quiet. I'm counting. Five. Six."

One hundred and sixty-seven trucks later, Michael was ready to scream. They stopped for lunch at a picnic table in a rest area. When they got going again, Norman started where he left off. "Hundred sixty-eight, hundred sixty-nine," he droned on.

When no trucks went by, Norman read the road signs out loud. "What's a facty outlet?" he asked.

"Factory outlet," said Mom. "That's a store where they sell things very cheaply. We have to stop there!"

The next sign said: CLOTHING, RUGS, POTTERY, BAS-KETS, LINENS, SHOES, SOCKS, FOUR MILES AHEAD.

"Socks!" exclaimed Michael.

"Maybe their prices are cheaper than the Save-A-Lot," said Dad.

As they turned off the highway at the one-mile-to-go sign, Norman told Fluffy, "We're going to a socks factory outlet. Maybe they have some new flavors you'll like."

"Amazing," said Michael when they entered the vast warehouse with aisles and aisles of socks as far as they could see.

Mom looked at some price tags. "These are much cheaper than Save-A-Lot. We'd better stock up."

"You mean sock up," said Norman, chuckling at his own joke.

A big sign said: TREAT YOUR TOOTSIES TO THE WORLD'S FINEST FOOTWEAR. Another said: WE HAVE YOUR SIZE—FROM BABY FEET TO BIG FOOT.

Off they went with shopping carts in four different directions.

Dad came back with several pairs of beige ones whose label said their color was oatmeal.

Mom came back with a package of tiny pink baby

38

socks. "For desserts," she joked. "Actually these are so cute I couldn't resist them. Maybe I can give them to someone for a baby present."

Michael came back with neon colors, orange and lime. "If the plants eat these, maybe they'll glow in the dark a little, like very big night-lights," he suggested.

"Try that," Dad said, "and you'll walk home from Florida."

Norman returned with the usual flavor colors—vanilla, chocolate, strawberry, and fudge ripple. He also had some pale green for mint and white with red stripes for cherry vanilla. He held up his best find, white socks with brown polka dots. "Chocolate chip!" he exclaimed.

Then he held up one more pair, red with white and green reindeer all over them.

"No," Mom said.

"Not for the plants," said Norman. "For a Christmas present."

"Nobody wants to wear socks like that," said Dad.

"Wait till you hear them," Norman said.

"Not *talking* socks!" said Mom.

Norman fumbled around with one sock and pressed something. With a tinkling music box sound, it began playing "Jingle Bells."

Michael read the label. "It has a microchip and a teeny battery," he explained. "Like that card Grandma sent me last year that plays 'Happy Birthday.' "

"Cute," Mom said. "You can turn it off now."

"How?" said Norman, pressing the sock again to no avail.

Michael looked at the label again. "You can't turn it off. It stops by itself when it gets to the end of the song." He told Norman, "Don't you dare give me those socks for Christmas!"

"Don't worry," said Norman. "They're not for you."

Mom said, "It's sweet of you to think of Christmas so early, Norman, but I really would rather have something else other than musical socks. *Anything* else."

Dad said, "Those aren't my style, either."

"Don't worry," Norman replied. "I already know who I'm giving them to, and it's not any of you."

"Who?" they all asked.

"Me," said Norman with a happy grin.

Chapter 8

Back on the highway, Norman started again on "How many more miles?" They all got so tired of it that Mom finally said, "I'd rather listen to you sing."

"Let's all sing," said Dad. He was now in a very good mood because they were almost to Florida. "When I was a kid, we always sang 'Row, Row, Row Your Boat' on trips."

Michael sighed. They had been through this before on long trips. But it was better than listening to Norman.

They all sang "Row, Row, Row Your Boat" four times and got the parts all mixed up. Then Dad told everybody else to pick a song.

Mom chose "Oh, Susanna." When they got to the part about "banjo on my knee," she pulled Norman over sideways on her lap and pretended to play his ribs like a banjo. This tickled, so he giggled the rest of the song instead of singing.

Michael refused to pick a song, so it was Norman's turn. He led them in singing "Jingle Bells," with musical backup by his reindeer sock.

Soon after that, they passed the sign that said: WEL-COME TO FLORIDA, THE SUNSHINE STATE. They all cheered.

Late in the day they finally turned into the campground drive. Norman shouted, "We're here! We're here!" Michael felt just as excited.

Dad went in the office to register. A man led the way to their campsite in a golf cart. They passed many rows of all kinds of RVs parked under tall trees. Families were cooking out, eating at picnic tables, or relaxing in lawn chairs. Kids were riding bikes on a paved bike path and climbing and swinging on a playground. The turquoise-blue swimming pool looked very inviting. Bathing suits and towels hung from clotheslines.

The man pointed out a low building where they could use washers and dryers. It also had showers and toilets for people who didn't have them in their RVs, plus snack machines and a day-care center.

Since this was their first time at a campground, the man helped them hook up their electricity, water, and sewer connections. Then he asked what those things sticking out of the roof were.

"Our pet plants," explained Norman.

They took the plants' traveling plastic wrappers off and ate dinner outside. Other families came over to say hello and ask where they were from. Everyone remarked about the plants sticking out of the roof. Some people driving along the road slowed down to look and point.

As it grew dark, they sat in their lawn chairs talking about what they were going to do tomorrow at Disney World.

The boys did not need to be told twice to go to bed. "The sooner you go to sleep, the sooner we go to Disney World in the morning," Mom reminded them.

Michael put a dirty sock next to Stanley. Norman put out a clean cherry vanilla one for Fluffy. Michael got his blanket and pillow for the couch, then Dad gave Norman a boost into the bunk.

The night was growing chilly, so Michael kept his socks on. The other time he slept on the couch, the blankets pulled up during the night and his feet stuck out and got cold.

Long after everyone went to sleep, Stanley reached for his sock meal. His vine wrapped around it and lifted it to one of his ice-cream-cone–shaped leaves, which sucked it in with a slow *schlurrrp*. Soon Fluffy did the same.

Michael stirred a little when he heard one of the plants burp as usual, but he woke up when something tugged at his foot. It took a moment for him to realize that Stanley had wrapped a vine around it.

"Quit that!" he said. "I'm not in the mood for tickling. I need a good night's sleep. We're going to Disney World tomorrow."

Then he realized that Stanley was not tickling. Stanley was tugging his sock off. Before he could grab it, the sock was whisked away. "Hey!" protested Michael.

There was a moment of silence. Then, in the dark, he heard the familiar *schlurrrp*.

What was going on? He turned on a light. The dirty sock he put out for Stanley's meal was also gone. His plant had eaten twice. He was getting hungrier.

Michael plopped down on the couch to go back to sleep. As he was drifting off, he heard Stanley burp again.

Then there was another burp, followed by an "Ex." Fluffy had eaten another helping, too, but from where?

In the morning Michael told Norman what had happened. "We'd better start giving them an extra sock for dessert," said Norman.

After they got dressed, they went outside. A boy at the RV next door was looking around under a clothesline. "Do you see a sock anywhere?" he asked. "I left a pair on the line last night with my bathing suit and towels. Now one's missing. Maybe it blew away."

The other sock still on the line was white with brown stripes, Fluffy's favorite flavor.

Michael looked up at the roof. Last night all Fluffy's vines were inside. Now one was stretched out on the roof.

"Bad plant!" he scolded.

"What?" said the boy.

"Nothing," said Michael. "We got lots of socks at a factory outlet store. We can give you a pair just like that one if you want."

"Thanks anyway," said the boy. "I've got plenty more."

Michael and Norman did not notice the seed pod that Fluffy had plucked off himself. It was nestled too deep in the underbrush where he had thrown it.

Chapter 9

Right after breakfast they set out for Disney World in the car Mom and Dad had rented so they wouldn't have to unhook the RV's electricity, water, and sewer connections every time they wanted to go somewhere.

Norman was so excited that whenever he tried to talk all he could do was squeak.

"Settle down," advised Dad. "We're going to spend five days there, so let's relax."

Disney World was just as great as the boys had imagined it would be. Their favorite ride was Space Mountain. Even though Michael felt as if he'd left his stomach behind on every plunge, he wanted to go again when it was over. So they did.

Among the many delights of the park, Norman was especially interested in the mechanical singing plants in the Enchanted Tikki Room Show. "I think they're related to Fluffy," he said.

Michael was fascinated by the futuristic plant-growing methods at Epcot.

They all got their pictures taken with Mickey. Norman got his taken with Goofy, too. "A perfect pair," said Michael.

One day Norman brought along his gorilla head and walked around with it on for a while. Little kids came up and hugged him, and their parents took their pictures with him.

"Great," said Dad. "Pictures of our son the gorilla head are going to be in family photo albums all over America."

Mom made him take the gorilla head off, but sometimes when she and Dad were walking ahead, he would pop it back on for a few minutes. Michael walked as far away from him as possible so nobody would know they were related.

There was so much to do and see that every evening they returned to the campground happy and exhausted. The first night Norman told Fluffy about Space Mountain and the singing plants, but he was too tired to talk anymore.

The second night all he said to Fluffy was "Hi" before he climbed into his bunk and konked out. Michael put the meals out for both plants and went right to sleep, too.

In the dark Stanley reached out and put a vine on Michael's shoulder, like a person who puts an arm around a friend. But Michael did not notice. He was sound asleep, dreaming of Disney World.

Next morning, as they were leaving again for the park, Mom remarked, "The plants look a little droopy. Did you guys water them?"

"I forgot," said Michael.

"Me, too," said Norman.

"Hurry up and do it," she said.

"We can do it later," Michael said. He was in a hurry to get to Disney World.

"Now," Mom insisted. She ran a finger across Fluffy's leaves. "This plant is dusty."

"I'll dust him later," said Norman, giving Fluffy a few quick squirts with his Water Blaster.

When they got back that night, the plants still looked droopy, but they did not notice. Norman didn't even bother to say "Hi" to Fluffy because he was so entranced with what they had seen and done at Disney World that day. The whole family sat outside talking about it until bedtime.

They slept so soundly that they did not hear the rain start before dawn. Soon it was pouring, drenching the tops of the plants above the roof, dripping down the leaves inside and splattering on the plastic floor covering.

Stanley stretched a couple of vines over the kitchen counter so the ends hung right over Michael's face. Drops of rain rolled off the leaves, down the vines, and went drip, drip, drip on his nose.

That woke him up. At first he thought Norman had gone berserk with his Water Blaster. When he sat up, he put his feet down right into a large, cold puddle.

He woke everybody else up because he didn't want to clean the whole mess up by himself. It took all their towels to mop up. They hauled the plants outside so the plastic floor covering could get completely dry. By then it had stopped raining. Mom made the boys haul the wet towels to the laundry room.

As they sat listening to three dryers full of towels rumble, Michael remarked, "At least we don't have to water the plants today."

Norman wandered outside to see what the kids at the day-care center were doing on the playground.

47

When the dryers stopped, Michael put the towels in the laundry baskets and went to find Norman. He was having a wonderful time in a circle with the other kids doing the hokey-pokey.

They were starting the last part where you put your whole self in. When they finished putting their whole selves in and out and shaking "all about," the game dissolved in laughter.

Michael called to Norman, "We have to go now."

The woman in charge and all the kids waved good-bye.

When the boys got back to the RV with the towels, Mom said, "The plastic is dry now. We can lug the plants back in."

Michael wanted to get going. "Let's leave them outside," he said. "They look like they need more sun."

"They do still look droopy," agreed Dad, "but leaving them out alone would not be a good idea."

"Maybe we could hire a baby-sitter," said Michael.

Mom said, "Go ask around the neighbors if any of them aren't going anywhere today. Maybe someone would be willing to keep an eye on them."

Michael did not want to go around asking the neighbors. "Let's take them to the day-care center," he said.

Dad and Michael rolled the plants along the paved bike path over to the playground.

Dad introduced himself to the woman in charge. "I know this is a strange request," he said, "but we'd like to leave our plants outside today to get some sun while we're at Disney World. They're looking a little droopy from being inside the RV too much. But we don't want to leave them out alone. Could we pay you something to keep them here? You wouldn't have to watch them every minute. Just make sure nobody walks off with them."

"Walks off with those?" asked the woman, staring up at the towering plants.

"They're very unusual plants," said Dad. "They won't be any trouble. They'll just stand there."

"Well, I suppose I'd have to charge our regular hourly rate per child, minus the cost of lunch. They don't eat lunch, do they?" she joked.

"Never lunch," said Dad.

"Of course, we can't be responsible if anything happens. Our insurance only covers humans."

"OK," said Dad.

"And you'll have to pick them up by six," she added. "Our day-care program closes then. If you're going to be late, we can arrange a reliable baby-sitter."

"Don't worry," said Dad. "We'll be back by six."

They jogged back to the campsite. Mom and Norman were waiting in the car. "Disney World, here we come!" said Mom, and off they went.

They had another wonderful day, even though they started a little late. Even on this fifth day, they all wanted to stay a little longer.

Dad said, "We have to pick up the plants at six."

"We've got plenty of time," said Mom. Then they found themselves inching along in rush-hour traffic.

"We're going to be late," said Dad.

Chapter 10

Michael tried not to worry. He sat in the backseat with what could happen to the plants running through his mind. They could get stolen. Some kid could take them home. They could get locked up in the day-care room all night with no socks to eat.

They arrived a half hour late. The playground was deserted except for a teenaged boy bouncing a basketball.

"Have you seen a couple of tall plants?" asked Dad. The boy glanced around at all the greenery surrounding the playground. "Are you kidding?" he asked.

"Two very large plants in pots on skateboards," Dad explained.

"Nope," said the boy, looking at them strangely.

They looked in the windows of the locked day-care room and checked the open rooms in the building. No plants.

They drove back to the campground gate and asked the man on duty if two large plants on rollers had gone out the gate with anyone.

"No," said the man, looking at them strangely.

"Then they have to be in the campground some-where," said Dad.

The man asked, "Are you by any chance the people with plants sticking out of your roof?"

"That's us."

"I've heard about you. Everybody's been going around all week asking each other if they saw that RV. You're sort of a landmark. Some visitors came in this afternoon to see friends who told them they were the fourth RV west of the one with the funny plants sticking out of the roof."

"Today they weren't sticking out," said Mom.

"Then no wonder they got lost. They drove around the whole campground at five miles an hour three times before they came back here for directions. So what's the problem with the plants?"

Dad explained about leaving them at the day-care center to get some sun and then getting back too late.

"Don't worry. Addie either took them home with her or got a baby-sitter for them. That's what she does when parents are late. She always leaves a note on your RV to let you know where to pick them up."

They went back to their campsite. Taped to the door was a note from Addie, saying she had taken the plants home with her and would keep them overnight. They could pick them up at the playground tomorrow.

Norman said, "They might eat her socks tonight."

Mom started organizing dinner, while Dad and the boys drove back to ask the gatekeeper where Addie lived. He drew them a little map of how to find her home, about a mile from the playground. They set off, with Michael holding the map.

"We turn left here?" asked Dad.

Michael looked at the map. "Right," he agreed. Dad turned right. The road dead-ended at a swamp. Dad turned the car around back to where they turned wrong and tried the opposite direction.

"You told me to turn the wrong way!" said Dad, very irritated.

"No," said Michael.

"But we should have turned left," Dad insisted.

"Right," agreed Michael.

"No," said Dad. "Left."

"Yes," Michael replied. "Left is right!"

Norman piped up from the backseat, "Let's try straight ahead and see where that goes."

Dad snatched the map from Michael. "Everybody just shut up!" he said.

"I didn't do anything," Norman whined indignantly. "So I shouldn't have to shut up!"

Dad stopped the car, turned around, and glared at him. Norman shut up. They soon arrived at Addie's house. "Can I stop shutting up now?" asked Norman. Dad sighed.

Addie invited them in. "I hoped I could keep the plants tonight," she said. "They're great to have around, and I'd love to have them at the day-care center every day as long as you're staying at the campground. Free of charge, of course."

Stanley and Fluffy looked so much better than they had in the morning.

"The children just loved them," Addie continued. "We rolled them into the middle of the playground and danced and sang around them."

"Sang?" asked Norman.

52

"Yes, I know this sounds silly, but the plants really seemed to like that, especially the smaller one. Of course, I've heard about how plants thrive if you talk or sing to them, but I never really believed that until today."

"What songs did you sing?" asked Norman.

" 'Ring Around the Rosey,' 'London Bridge,' and 'The Hokey Pokey.' "

"Is that the one," asked Dad, "where you put your whole self in and shake it all about?"

"That's it."

"I used to love that one when I was little," said Dad. This was news to Michael. He hoped Dad would not start doing the Hokey Pokey, at least not until they got back to their RV where nobody would see him.

"The plants look much healthier than they did this morning," observed Dad. "Maybe all that attention from the kids today was good for them, along with the sunshine."

Michael felt guilty. He had been neglecting Stanley, just throwing socks down in front of him every night and ignoring him the rest of the time because he was having such a good time at Disney World.

Norman must have felt guilty, too, because he threw his arms around Fluffy and started humming softly.

"That boy really loves his plant," said Addie. "If you have to take them back to your RV tonight, can we have them again tomorrow? I promised the children I would ask."

They said that would be fine. "Now we have to get going," said Dad. "My wife will be wondering what happened to us."

Addie said, "I'm sorry my husband isn't here. He hauled the plants home in his pickup truck, but he's driven it to a meeting and won't be home until late. I don't see how you can get them in your car."

"No," said Dad, "we'll have to roll them on the bike path. I'll drive back and get my wife while the boys get started. She can bring me back to help them."

They lugged the plants out of Addie's house. Dad gave Michael the map and told them to get going. He drove off.

The boys waved good-bye to Addie. "I'll see you tomorrow." she called. They set off pushing the plants along the narrow bike path that ran beside the dirt road.

It was slow going. First they grabbed the main stalks and walked next to the plants, pulling them along. Although they were securely fastened to the skateboards, the plants were heavy and awkward to move a long way. If they got too close to the path's edge, they would go off and might tip over.

"Hurry up," said Norman. "I'm getting tired."

"I'm going as fast as I can," Michael replied, who was leading the way. His arms were starting to feel strained from pulling, so he got behind Stanley to push for a while.

They did not hear the bicycles coming up behind them until the riders yelled, "Out of the way!" The boys shoved the skateboards right to the edge, and the bikes whizzed by. One rider yelled back, "No skateboarding on the bike path!"

"We're not skateboarding!" shouted Michael. But the cyclists were gone around a bend.

Fluffy's back wheels had slid off the paved edge. Norman was struggling to get them back on. Michael turned back and helped him get Fluffy rolling again. They pushed for a long time. It was getting dark. The

54

path was farther from the road now, turning into the woods.

Michael stopped to look at the map, which was for the road, not the bike path. Dad and Mom should have come by a long time ago. If the boys got too far from the road, they might not be able to see them.

"Maybe we should stop here and wait for them," said Michael.

"I'm hungry," Norman complained.

Michael was hungry, too. Maybe there was something wrong with the car. Or maybe Dad turned the wrong way again and got lost without the map. He was sure the bicycle path came out eventually in the campground. One part of it went right past their RV. Besides, they could not roll the plants on the bumpy dirt road.

He explained all this to Norman. They decided to keep going.

Michael pushed Stanley faster, but Norman was falling behind, so he slowed up and let Norman push ahead with Fluffy.

As they moved on through the trees, it was darker and hard to see the edges of the path. The wheels went off a couple of times. It took both of them to get them back up on the pavement.

It seemed as if they had been pushing plants for hours. "Have you got your Mickey Mouse watch on?" Michael asked.

"Yeah," replied Norman, "but it's so dark I can't see what numbers Mickey's hands are pointing to. You don't think we're lost, do you?"

Michael was wondering the same thing. "How could we be lost?" he answered. "We're still on the bike path."

There was a pause. The sound of Norman's feet and Fluffy's rollers on the path stopped. Then Norman said "No, we're not."

"What are you talking about?" asked Michael. He felt Stanley bump over the edge and pull out of his hands. He also heard gooshy noises.

"I know where we are," said Norman.

"Where?" asked Michael, stepping along to retrieve Stanley. Where he stepped his feet sank into chilly goo up to his ankles.

"We're in the swamp," said Norman.

Chapter 11

"Now don't panic," said Michael, who was starting to panic. "We just have to think up a master plan to get out of here and find Mom and Dad." He reached out, found Stanley, and pulled. But the plant was sunk up to its pot in the swamp and did not budge.

The dim outlines that were all he could see of Norman and Fluffy looked shorter than usual. "Are you sinking?" he asked, trying to sound calm.

"Not anymore," replied Norman. "I think I'm sunk as far as I'm going to sink. It's only up to my knees." Then he added in a quavery voice, "You don't think this is quicksand, do you? Like in that movie?"

"No, of course not. What movie?"

"*The Swamp Monster*. Remember we stayed up to watch it one time Mom and Dad were out late and the baby-sitter fell asleep?"

Michael remembered. Mom would never let them watch that one even when it was on during the day, because she saw it when she was a kid and it gave her nightmares.

"Remember," Norman continued, "the monster was

57

a big bunch of walking swamp glop? You don't think this glop I'm standing in can get up and walk, do you?''

"Stop it!" Michael said sharply. "You'll scare yourself silly." And, he thought, me, too.

He tried to think of something calm to say. "The monster was just some guy in a glop suit. It wasn't real. It was special effects.''

"Then when he got sucked down into the quicksand," said Norman, "he wasn't really dead? He could come back?''

"Stop it!" said Michael. "We have to do something, not just stand around in the mud talking. Monsters and quicksand are not the problem.''

"What about alligators?" Norman asked. "There were big ones in the movie.''

"Forget alligators," said Michael. "Try to lift a foot.''

He tried lifting one of his own and it came out of the goo. He lifted the other one and kept going backward until he found the paved path and got up on it.

"I got one foot out," reported Norman from the darkness, "but the glop sucked my sock and shoe off.''

"Never mind," said Michael, "keep coming toward the sound of my voice.''

"I don't want to put my foot back in the goo.''

"You have to. You can't hop out of there on one foot.''

"This is disgusting," Norman said as he dipped his toes back in. "And cold. Yech!" Still trying to stand on one foot, he lost his balance and fell—*splat*!—backward into the swamp glop.

Michael saw the dim form of his brother go over and jumped back into the swamp. "Give me your hand!" he yelled.

"Oh, yuck," Norman said and reached out. After a

few misses in the dark, Michael found Norman's slimy little hand and pulled him upright.

"Now keep going," he instructed, clutching Norman's hand and trying to drag him along faster.

"Not so fast," protested Norman. "The mud is sucking off my other sock and shoe. And it's my microchip sock!"

"Let it go," said Michael impatiently. Since he was taller, the mud did not come up so far on him, and he could go faster. He yanked at Norman, but his hand slipped away and—*splat!*— Norman fell face-down into the swamp glop.

Michael found his hand again, wiped the slime off with the bottom of his T-shirt, and pulled Norman upright. Norman sputtered and kept spitting to get the mud off his mouth.

"I'll get you for that," he said angrily.

"I'm saving you, so shut up!" snarled Michael. He kept pulling, slower this time, and dragged Norman up on the path.

"You made me fall on my face," Norman accused him.

"I did not!"

They sat down on the path, oozing goo, Michael from the shins down, and Norman from head to toes.

"We can't get the plants out without help," said Michael. "We can walk back to Addie's if we just follow the path. We can use her phone to call the camp gate and get the man there to help us find Mom and Dad."

"Shhh," said Norman. "I hear something."

It was a car, getting closer. Then they saw headlights coming up to a nearby edge of the swamp.

"Let's yell 'help' together," said Norman.

"It looks like a pickup truck," said Michael. "Wait till we see if we can tell who it is," he cautioned. "We don't want to yell if they're crooks or something."

"I don't care," Norman said. "I'm yelling anyway."

As he took a deep breath to start, Michael put a hand over his mouth. In the silence they heard a familiar voice from the open windows of the truck.

"Our kids are lost," said Mom loudly, "and you insisted on turning the wrong way, and now we're lost ourselves in this dumb swamp!"

The boys started yelling: "Mom! Dad! Help! Over here!"

"There they are!" Mom shouted. "We're coming!" The truck backed up and turned slowly so the headlights swept across the swamp.

Suddenly revealed in the bright lights were Michael, waving, and just behind him, with arms outstretched, a small but horrible creature made of walking swamp glop.

Mom screamed, but then she quickly realized that this must be Norman.

The truck came around the edge of the swamp and parked near the boys with the headlights shining on them. Their parents jumped out and hugged them, glop and all.

The boys told them what happened. "What took you so long?" Michael asked. "And where did you get the truck?"

Dad explained that when he got back to the RV Mom was not there. He went around to neighboring RVs to ask if anyone had seen her. When he realized he'd wasted twenty minutes looking, he walked down the campground road yelling her name. People looked at him strangely, but Mom heard him and came out of an RV where she'd been visiting.

It was beginning to get dark, so they decided to try to borrow a pickup truck. That way they could drive the plants back quicker than it would take to roll them in the dark. Finding someone willing to lend a truck took more time. Then they took some wrong turns because Dad had given the map to Michael.

Mom looked at her muddy children. "You better ride in the back of the pickup," she said. "Then we can hose it down before we return it, and you, too."

Michael reminded her, "First we have to get the plants out."

"You better glue your shoes on first," warned Norman, pointing to his mud-slathered bare feet.

"Not your expensive running shoes!" Mom exclaimed.

"Yep," Norman replied, "and my reindeer socks, too."

"Well, we can get along without those," Dad said. "Let's drive back and see if we can borrow some fishing boots to wade in there. Or, better still, let's come back in the morning to pry them out when we can see better."

Norman wailed, "I'm not leaving Fluffy alone out here in a swamp! The alligators might get him!"

"Calm down," Dad said. "Fluffy won't be alone. Stanley is here to keep him company. And I'm sure alligators don't eat plants."

Mom turned toward the plants, which looked bright green in the headlights. "They look right at home in a swamp," she said.

"Look!" exclaimed Michael. Stanley's two thickest vines were sunk in the mud and moving.

Stanley slowly pulled his vines out of the mud. The

ends were wrapped tightly around two big muddy lumps. From one gooey bundle, very faintly, came the tinkling sound of "Jingle Bells."

"My socks and shoes!" yelped Norman. He was so excited he slogged back into the swamp. "Thanks, Stanley," he said as he unwrapped the vines. He hugged the big plant and squished his way back to firm ground.

Michael grinned. "Stanley will go for dirty socks anywhere," he boasted. Norman asked Dad to pull the microchip and battery out of his sock before the wet mud soaked all the way through and ruined them. Dad extracted them and put them away in his wallet.

"Get in the truck," commanded Mom. "Right now."

Michael still felt guilty about neglecting his plant ever since they got to Florida. "I'm not leaving without Stanley," he said, "and Norman's not leaving without Fluffy!"

"Yeah," said Norman.

"We'll get them later," Dad said.

"No," said Michael. "If the plants don't go with us now, Norman and I will spend the night here."

"Wait a minute!" squawked Norman.

"And you can't leave your lost children alone in the swamp," Michael added, "so you'll have to stay here with us!"

"Yeah," Norman chimed in. He raised his muddy arms and walked stiff-legged toward Mom. He warned, "And maybe the swamp monster will get us!"

Mom jumped back. "Well," she said, "we've already got some mud on us from hugging you. I guess a little more won't hurt." She took off her shoes and socks and rolled her jeans up to her knees.

Dad did the same. The four of them, with a lot of

hearty heave-hos, got Fluffy and Stanley hoisted out of the goo and into the back of the truck.

Mom and Dad had mud up to their shins and elbows, plus plenty more smeared and splashed on the rest of them. "You should ride in the back, too," said Norman.

"Somebody has to drive," Mom pointed out. She used her socks to wipe most of the mud off her feet and hands and got behind the wheel.

The boys and Dad climbed into the back and sat down, holding on to the sides. Mom gunned the motor. "Ready back there?" she yelled. "All set!" yelled Dad. "Blast off!" yelled Norman. "Five, four, three, two . . ." He never got to one. Mom took off, bumping toward the road, and the plants took off, too, rolling all over the truck bed. They thudded into the far end, which hurled them back toward their three startled companions.

"Grab them!" yelled Dad. They tackled the rolling pots. Dad pounded on the back of the truck cab. "Slow down!" he shouted. "Or we'll get run over by speeding plants!"

Mom slowed down to a creep. Dad and the boys shoved the plants up against the back of the truck cab and sat down in front of them. They linked arms to keep the plants from getting loose.

After a few wrong turns on unlighted back roads, they saw streetlights ahead and turned onto a paved street.

They stopped at a gas station to find out where they were and get gas, so they could return the truck with a full tank.

As the attendant gave them directions, he stared at the tall plants with muddy pots and smiled at Norman's head-to-toe goo. "Who's your little mudman here?" he asked. "You must be a new character trying to get a job at Disney World."

Norman liked that idea, so he smiled back. That made the dried mud covering his face crack all over his cheeks and forehead. Now he looked even stranger.

"Want to sell these plants?" the man asked.

"I'd love to," said Mom, "but unfortunately we can't right now."

When Dad went to pay for the gas, he patted his back pocket where his wallet was before he pulled it out. It started playing "Jingle Bells." It kept on playing while he took the money out and waited for the change.

"Want to sell that wallet?" asked the attendant. "My kid would love that." Dad said no, and they drove off with the wallet still playing. Norman sang along.

Chapter 12

When they got back to the campground, Mom told the man at the gate, "That swamp you have is a hazard to people and plants!"

"We don't have a swamp," said the gateman. "You must be talking about that little mud hole out in the woods. It's sort of a nature preserve."

"Ha!" Mom replied. "I've seen swamps in the movies, and I know one when I step in it! It's a swamp!"

Instead of stopping at their RV, she drove directly to the building where the showers were. "This mud is too much for the little shower in our RV," she explained. "Bring the plants."

Michael started to take off his muddy shoes and socks. "Leave them on," said Mom. "Leave everything on. Just empty your pockets."

They all got into shower stalls with their clothes on and kept turning around in the spray until most of the mud was rinsed off. Norman came out looking like himself again.

Then they rolled the plants into shower stalls and rinsed their pots and skateboards.

As they were going out, a woman carrying a basket of clean clothes out of the laundry room stopped at the sight of them. "The weather report didn't say anything about rain tonight," she said. "You really got caught in a downpour! The dryer makes so much noise I guess I didn't hear the storm."

"Uh . . . yes, well, it's not raining now," Dad assured her.

Back at the RV, Dad and the boys hoisted the plants in while Mom returned the truck. They changed their wet clothes for pajamas and heated up the dinner Mom had fixed earlier.

After they ate, the boys put socks out for the plants. Norman sang quietly to Fluffy and hugged him. Michael patted Stanley's leaves and told him he wasn't going to ignore him anymore.

"Tomorrow, Cypress Gardens," Dad announced.

In the morning, they rolled the plants to the playground as promised. Mom sent Michael to the laundry room to wash and dry their still soggy clothes from last night.

"Why do I get stuck with this?" he complained. "How come Norman gets to stay here and play while I have to do the laundry?"

"He's going to help me clean up and empty the trash," said Mom.

"But that's not fair. He likes to clean up! Why does he get to do something he likes?"

"Would you rather clean up?" she asked.

"Nope," he said grumpily.

"If I needed somebody to make a really good mess, I'd ask you to handle it. But I need to clean up now while the plants are out of the way. Take a book along.

You'll be done before you know it." She stuck a plastic bottle of detergent on top of the clothes basket and opened the door for him.

Michael trudged toward the laundry room, past the playground. Stanley and Fluffy were surrounded by little kids doing the Hokey Pokey. Michael couldn't figure out why the plants looked so much better, but they seemed to be standing straighter, with their vines and leaves lifted, almost as if they were feeling happier.

He stuffed the clothes into a washer and followed the directions about how to turn it on. He had forgotten to bring a book, so he went outside to watch the kids.

Now they were playing follow the leader, pretending to be plants. Addie was leading, pushing Fluffy. "Wave your vines," she called out, and they all waved their arms. Stanley stood off to one side. Michael could not be sure, but he thought he saw Stanley's vines move ever so slightly.

"Wiggle your leaves," called Addie. They all wiggled their arms and legs and heads and giggled. Stanley's leaves rustled as if there were a little breeze. Michael hoped it was only a breeze.

"Spin around on your skateboards," called Addie, pushing Fluffy in a circle. The children turned around and around. Was Stanley leaning back and forth to try to get his skateboard rolling?

Michael ran over and grabbed Stanley. "Hi," said Addie. "Children, this is Michael. These plants belong to him and his little brother. You already know Norman."

A little girl said shyly, "I love your plant." Another said, "I love both of them!" Everybody started to talk at once.

Michael tightened his grip on Stanley. "I'm going to take my plant into the laundry room," he said.

"Why?" asked a little boy.

"This plant is sort of my friend—like a pet—and I haven't spent much time with him—it—lately because we've been going to Disney World."

"Are you going to sing?" asked someone else. "It likes when we sing."

"No," Michael replied. "I'll just let it listen to the washer and dryer."

He pushed on. When he got far enough from the children so they would not hear him, he muttered, "Come on, Stanley, you can't do things where people can see you."

"Is that its name?" asked a small boy he had not noticed following him. "Stanley?"

"Well, uh, yeah."

"What's the other one named?" asked a very small girl he also had not noticed.

He whispered to her so no one would hear, "Fluffy."

"Fuffy!" she mispronounced with a shout and ran off to hug Fluffy. "Its name is Fuffy!" she called to everyone.

"Fuffy! Fuffy!" shouted all the other children, hopping around the plant.

Back in the laundry room, Michael found a girl about his own age putting clothes into a washing machine.

"Hi," she said.

"Hi," he replied.

"We just got here last night," she said.

"We've been here five days," he said. He tried to think of something else to say. But, of course, when Stanley or Fluffy was around, people always had something to say.

"That's a great plant," she said. "Do you take it with you everywhere?"

68

"No, mostly it stays home. We decided to bring it along on vacation because it needs special care."

She looked closely at Stanley. "My mom would really like to see this plant," she said. "Would you watch my wash while I go and get her?"

"Sure, I guess," he replied. Her mother must be some kind of a plant nut. Practically everyone in the campground had already seen the plants, so one more would not matter.

While she was gone, the machine with Michael's wash clunked to a stop. He put the wet clothes into a dryer and turned it on.

As he waited, he decided that maybe singing to Stanley would be a good idea, sort of like spending quality time with him. All he could think of was the words to "Jingle Bells," so he sat down next to Stanley and sang very quietly. He got the feeling Stanley liked that.

Hearing footsteps, he stopped. The girl was back with her mother, who looked a lot like Michael's mother and was wearing jeans, running shoes, and a red T-shirt that said Save The Rain Forests.

The woman looked excited when she saw Stanley. "Where did you get this plant?" she asked.

"I grew it," he said.

"Where did you get the seed? Or was it a cutting?" she asked.

Michael did not want to go into details about Stanley. "Why do you want to know?" he asked.

"I'm a botanist," she replied. Michael looked at her blankly because he didn't know what that was. She added, "A scientist who specializes in plants."

Chapter 13

The woman's daughter explained, "Botany is from the Latin word *botanicus*. That means plant."

"Oh," said Michael.

"I'm going to be a botanist, too," said the girl. "What are you going to be?"

"I haven't decided yet," he said.

"You like plants," she said, "so maybe you'll be a botanist, too."

Her mother said, "You've certainly taken good care of this one. Sarah, you were right. This plant is very unusual. I'll have to do some research to find out what species it is." She handed Michael one of her business cards. It said: *Susan Sparks, Ph.D.*

"Research?" said Michael. He did not like the sound of that. "Thanks, that's really nice of you, but I don't want any research."

"Don't you want to know what species it is? You may have something really rare here," said Dr. Sparks. She noticed his worried look. "I won't hurt your plant.

I only want to identify it and observe what's special about it."

Michael just looked at her because he couldn't think how to answer.

"I'll be able to tell you what its scientific Latin name is," she added. "Wouldn't you like to know what your plant's name is?"

"No, thank you," said Michael.

"Why not? It'll be really interesting for you to know more about it."

"Um, I don't think my plant would like that."

"What do you mean?" asked Dr. Sparks, looking very interested. "Does it demonstrate some unusual behavior that makes you think it doesn't like certain things?"

"No."

"Then how can you tell? Or does it manifest some unusual reaction that may indicate it has an affinity for certain environments?"

"What?" said Michael.

"She means," translated Sarah, "does it do anything to show it likes something?"

Michael felt backed into a corner with this question. "Do anything?" he repeated, stalling for time to think.

"You know," said Sarah, "the way plants turn their leaves toward the sunlight. Of course, they do that so slowly that we don't notice them moving."

"Yes, it does that in the daytime," Michael said. He wasn't going to tell them how fast Stanley moved toward dirty socks during the night.

"What's your campsite number?" asked Dr. Sparks. "I'd like to speak to your parents."

71

"I can't remember," he said, "and I have to go now." He looked at the timer on the dryer. It had ten minutes to go, but he turned it off and pulled the still-damp clothes out into the basket.

Lugging the heavy basket with one arm and pushing Stanley with the other, he struggled out the door.

Dr. Sparks told Sarah, "I'll stay with the wash. Go along and help him with the clothes basket. Since he doesn't remember his campsite number, he can show you where it is."

Now Michael was really stuck. There was no escape from these botany people!

"Let me have the basket," Sarah said. He protested, but she insisted. He finally let her have it, because it needed two hands to carry it, and he was about to drop it any minute.

"These clothes aren't dry," she said.

"My family doesn't like clothes that are too dry," he said.

"That's odd," commented Sarah.

"Yeah," he agreed.

Suddenly the little boy who had followed him before came around the corner of the building from the playground. "Hi, Stanley," he said, waving at the plant.

Michael waved back.

They walked on in silence. Michael couldn't think of anything to say. He didn't want to explain about Stanley's name. Maybe she wouldn't ask.

He thought about stopping at somebody else's campsite to throw her off the track. But anybody in the campground could tell her where the RV with the plants sticking out was. So he stopped at the right one.

"My mom will be over," Sarah said, "but not today.

We're going to Cypress Gardens. We always go there when we come to Florida. They have eight thousand different kinds of plants.''

"That's a really big garden," said Michael.

"It's great," said Sarah. "You should go."

"Thanks for carrying the basket."

"That's OK," she said. "See you later."

He went into the RV and told Norman, "Help me get Stanley in."

"What did you bring him back for?" asked Norman.

"Maybe it was my imagination, but he sort of looked like he was going to start acting up on the playground—and now a botanist is after him to do research!"

"A what-in-ist?" asked Norman.

"A botanist," Michael said impatiently, pushing Stanley up the RV steps while Norman pulled. "You don't know what that is, do you?"

"I do, too," replied Norman. "It's somebody who likes bots."

Michael explained about Sarah and her mother.

Norman looked worried. "What about Fluffy? Are they after him, too?"

"They don't know yet that there's another one. They only saw Stanley. But they'll find out eventually. If they don't see Fluffy on the playground, they'll see both of them sticking out of the air vents."

Mom and Dad came in carrying groceries. "What's Stanley doing back here?" asked Dad.

Michael told them what happened.

"This could be trouble," said Dad.

"On the other hand," Mom said, "what harm would it do for a scientist to find out what kind of plants they are? If we knew more about them, maybe we could figure out how to make them stop eating socks."

"But," said Michael, "what if these are the only two plants like these in the whole world? Then scientists would be after them all the time."

"They'd be very valuable," Mom said. "We've only promised to keep them until after Pet Plant Day. Then maybe we can sell them for a lot of money."

"When they grow more pods, maybe we could sell some seeds to scientists," said Dad, "if they'd keep quiet about where they got them."

"I'm not selling Fluffy!" shouted Norman. "He's my friend!"

"Oh, Norman," Mom said, "you haven't paid any attention to that plant since we got to Florida."

He protested, "I pay attention to him now. I sang to him last night and everything."

Dad said, "Let's not get all upset and ruin our vacation over this. We're supposed to be relaxing and having a good time. No worrying or arguing. We can do that at home."

Michael said, "Letting a plant scientist study our plants will ruin my vacation!"

"Me, too!" Norman added. "It'll make me worry all the time!"

"All right," agreed Dad, "but how do we keep the botanist away? We're parked in a public place with the plants sticking out."

"We can ask Addie to keep them at her house," said Michael.

"Do you want to explain to her how to feed them socks at night?" Mom asked.

Michael said, "We could hide the tops on the roof so no one can see them stick out."

"How?" asked Dad.

74

Michael had no idea how.

"Put blankets over them," said Norman.

"We need all our blankets to sleep with," Mom said.

"Tablecloths," Norman said.

"We don't have any," said Mom.

"Let's buy some," Norman said. "Big, red-checked ones, so it'll look like we're having a picnic on the roof. We can put picnic tables over the tops of the plants and put the tablecloths on top of those."

"I think," said Dad, "that might attract just a little too much attention. Not to mention the crane we'd need to hoist the picnic tables up to the roof."

"And," Mom said, "the fact that the picnic tables would be so heavy they'd probably crash through the roof and destroy the RV and the plants and us, too."

Norman looked disappointed that they didn't like his idea.

"But," said Dad, "you're thinking creatively, son."

Norman beamed with pride. "I got another idea," he said.

Michael expected another crazy one, but Norman said, "We can put some of our bags and folded-up lawn chairs and stuff on the roof around the plant tops. Then nobody can see them, and they'll still get sunshine."

Michael was amazed. That would actually work. He said, "Lots of RVs have stuff on the roof."

Dad said, "But nearly everyone who's been camping here more than one day has seen the plants sticking out. And Sarah can show her mother where we are."

"Then," said Michael, "we have to do one more thing to make our disguise complete."

"What?" asked Mom.

"Disappear to another campsite!"

Norman headed for the playground to get Fluffy. Mom and Michael started gathering things to put on the roof. Dad went to the campground office to see if they could get another campsite.

It took a half hour to unhook the electricity, water, and sewer connections, and another half hour to hook up at their new campsite. There they sat disguised as an RV with a lot of stuff on its roof but no plants.

Chapter 14

"The morning is shot," Dad said over lunch, "so where do you want to go this afternoon?"

"Not Cypress Gardens," said Michael. "That's where Sarah and her mom went today. We better wait till tomorrow."

Dad spread some tourist brochures on the table among the sandwiches. Norman snatched one up and shouted, "Gatorland!" He looked at the pictures. "Giant alligators! Baby ones! Funny pink birds with long, skinny necks!"

"Flamingos," said Michael.

"Those, too," Norman said. "Look, you can get your picture taken with a little alligator and a big snake."

"That's a boa constrictor," said Michael.

"We'll skip that part." Mom said.

Norman told Fluffy where they were going and that they would be back in a few hours. He turned on Dad's little portable radio to keep the plants company because, he said, "Fluffy likes singing."

On the way to Gatorland Zoo, Michael told Norman, "I thought you were afraid of alligators."

"Not when they can't get me," replied Norman.

"He's right," Dad said. "They're very dangerous. A big one could kill you with one chomp, but this place is a safe way to see them."

Back at the RV, Fluffy and Stanley seemed to be enjoying the radio. They stood quietly rustling their leaves in time to the music.

Norman loved Gatorland's entrance. It was a giant green fake alligator head with its jaws open for you to walk through. Big white teeth stuck up from the bottom and down from the top. Michael thought it was pretty good, too.

They crossed a bridge over a lake full of huge alligators. "Look at that one," exclaimed Michael. "It's as long as a station wagon!" More rose to the surface of the water. They looked just as horrible as in movies or on TV, the only other places he had seen them.

They took a tour of the grounds on a little train and strolled on a wooden walkway through a swamp full of cypress trees. Mom said, "I like this swamp a lot better than the one we were in last night."

"I don't have to glue on my shoes in this one," said Norman.

"Stanley and Fluffy would like this swamp," said Michael. He was glad the plants were safe back in the RV, where they couldn't get into trouble.

Stanley and Fluffy were rustling their leaves slower for slow songs and faster for fast ones. When the radio started playing "Whole Lotta Shakin' Goin' On," they started shaking their leaves faster and faster until they were quivering violently all over. When that song ended, there was a commercial for Florida orange juice. The plants stopped shaking and sagged like tired dancers.

One of Stanley's vines felt its way over to the radio and tried to press the button to turn it off. When that didn't work, the vine wrapped around the little radio and banged it against the kitchen countertop. The radio played on.

So Stanley reached out a second vine, wrapped it around the handle of the refrigerator door, and yanked it open. His first vine dropped the little radio into a pitcher of orange juice. The music stopped.

Stanley raised the vine that had dipped into the juice to one of his ice-cream-cone–shaped leaves. He let the drops of juice fall into it.

If any people had been around, they would have heard a small murmur from Stanley that sounded a lot like "Mmmmm."

At the Gator Jumparoo Show, huge alligators were leaping four or five feet out of the water with snapping jaws to snatch chicken meat off a cable. The crowd oohed and clapped. Little children shrieked with excitement.

Afterward they went to the snack bar.

"We have to try a Gator Bite," said Dad.

"What is this?" Norman asked. "Something alligators eat?"

"Deep-fried morsels of tasty alligator tail," Dad read from the brochure.

"Their tails didn't look tasty to me," said Michael.

"How do you know if you don't try it?" Dad asked. "It'll be an adventure in eating."

"I'll have a salad," said Mom.

"Come on," Dad said, "how often do you get a chance to taste alligator meat?"

"Once is too often," Mom said.

Dad handed Michael a piece. Michael looked at it. "You try it first," he told Dad.

Dad took a very tiny bite and chewed. "Not bad," he said. "It tastes a little like chicken, but not exactly."

"No wonder," said Michael, "after all the chicken they eat in the Jumperoo Show." He decided to try a bite. Dad hadn't thrown up, so how bad could it be?

To get up his nerve, he thought about his friends asking, "What did you do on your vacation?" He could say casually, "I went on Space Mountain five times and ate tasty morsels of alligator tails." They would be very impressed.

He took a small bit. It was OK. It did taste sort of like chicken, but sort of like fish, too. He finished the piece.

"Ugh," said Norman. "Now alligator stuff is sliding down your insides to your stomach. Oooh, ehhhh!"

"Quit yapping and eat yours," Michael said irritably. "Then you can tell all your friends when we get home, and they'll be very impressed. Go ahead. It tastes chickeny and fishy at the same time."

Norman was feeling a little queasy from watching the alligators tear away at all that raw chicken in the show. He picked up a morsel of alligator meat and paused to get up his nerve. "Don't say chicken," he said.

So, of course, Michael waited until Norman was swallowing and then said, "Chicken, chicken, chicken."

Norman gagged and spit out the chewed alligator morsel.

"That's disgusting," Michael said.

"I told you not to say chicken!" said Norman angrily.

"I wouldn't have thought of it if you hadn't said don't say it," Michael snarled, trying to blame what he had done on Norman.

"Time out!" yelled Dad, making a referee's "T" signal with his hands. "That's enough! We're spending a lot of money on this vacation. You'd better behave and enjoy this, or else!"

"You didn't finish your alligator," Michael told Norman. Norman knocked his lemonade over. Most of it went on Michael's shirt.

"He did that on purpose!" complained Michael.

"Did not!" Norman said.

"Did too!"

"That's it," said Mom. "We're leaving."

"But we didn't see the baby alligators yet," Norman whined.

Mom stopped. "I did want to see those," she said. "Will you two promise to behave?"

They promised.

"It will be nice to get back to Fluffy and Stanley," she said. "They're much better behaved and peaceful than you two, at least during the day."

Back at the RV, the refrigerator door still stood open. Stanley was dipping several vines into the orange juice pitcher and then flicking drops at his leaves and going "Mmmmm" a lot. He was also accidentally flicking some drops on the floor and walls and ceiling, even as far as Fluffy. There was quite a bit of orange juice flying around.

Chapter 15

They all thought the baby alligators were really cute. Since Norman couldn't buy a real one, he got a good fake one, two feet long, at the gift shop. Michael bought some postcards with alligator pictures to send to Grandma, Chad, and Jason. Mom bought a foot-long alligator made of fudge to mail to Grandma. Dad didn't buy anything, because by the time he paid for what everyone else bought, he decided they had spent enough for that day.

On the way back to the campground, Mom said, "Since we had a late snack, I think I'll just fix some tuna-fish salad for dinner."

Norman was busy in the backseat pretending that his fake alligator was sneaking up on Dad.

"That would be better than alligator salad," said Michael.

Norman pounced his alligator on Dad's shoulder. "Not while I'm driving," Dad said.

Norman sneaked his alligator up behind Mom. "Not now, Norman," she said. She looked out at the passing scenery. "It'll be nice to get back to the RV and just relax for a while."

"I don't hear the radio," observed Michael as Dad unlocked the door. "Maybe it needs new batteries."

Mom raised a couple of shades to let daylight in. "Somebody's been in our refrigerator," she exclaimed, "and left the door open!"

"Somebody's been drinking our orange juice," said Norman, pointing to the half-empty pitcher.

Dad took out the pitcher and looked into it. "Somebody drowned my radio!" he said.

Norman peered cautiously into his bunk as if the juice-guzzler and radio-drowner might be up there. "Nobody's sleeping in my bed," he told Mom. "You better see if somebody's sleeping in your bed."

"We are not the three bears," replied Mom.

"I know that," Norman said. "There's four of us."

"Nobody could have gotten in," Dad said. "The lock wasn't tampered with."

Michael looked around carefully. He saw the orange drips on the window shades and more on the plastic sheet on the floor. He touched Stanley's leaves and vines. They felt sticky.

"Somebody's been throwing our orange juice around," he said, "and here he is!"

"Stanley?" said Mom.

"Are you sure?" asked Dad.

"Fluffy didn't do it," said Norman, even though he wasn't sure about that. "Fluffy would never do anything messy. He's neat like me."

"These plants are going to drive me crazy," said Mom. "And we're stuck with them until Pet Plant Day

83

next fall. Five minutes after that day is over, these plants are history!"

Michael ran water on two washcloths. He gave one to Norman and started wiping up sticky orange drips.

"I don't have to help," protested Norman. "My plant didn't make this mess."

"You're the neatness expert," Michael said. "You're better at cleaning up than anybody, even Mom."

"Now, wait a minute," said Mom.

"I hate to admit it," Michael told her, "but out of all the neat people I have ever known, Norman is the best."

"True," said Norman, looking pleased with himself.

Michael went on flattering him. "You're the only one who knows how to clean up the right way. I'm only an expert on making messes. You're the champion at cleaning up." He dabbed at a juice spatter with a corner of the washcloth. "Is this how to do this?" he asked.

Norman could not resist telling his older brother what to do. "No, this way!" he said, wiping in a big sweep.

Michael dabbed at another little drip. "You're not doing it right!" Norman exclaimed. In showing Michael how to do it over and over, he cleaned all the shades and walls, and went on to the couch and plastic floor covering.

"Keep rinsing your washcloth," commanded Norman. Michael rinsed. By the time he finished wiping up the small kitchen area around Stanley, Norman had done all the rest.

After dinner, the family went for a walk. Along the way they said hello to new families who had just arrived from Illinois, Kentucky, and New Hampshire. The boys told the new kids about the great things to see and do at Disney World and Gatorland.

When they got back to their RV after dark, Dad said, "Let's go to Cypress Gardens tomorrow, and tape the refrigerator door shut just in case."

Mom said, "I'll mix some more frozen orange juice in the morning. We can take what's left after breakfast along with us. That will be easier than taping up the refrigerator."

While Michael was waiting for Norman to finish getting ready for bed in the teeny bathroom, he told Mom, "Cypress Gardens has eight thousand kinds of plants."

Dad replied, "If they have that many, maybe they have one or two of the same kind as ours. There must be some more of these somewhere."

Norman marched out of the bathroom. "Next!" he said, and smiled warmly at Michael. Norman was in a very good mood. Maybe cleaning made him a nicer person, thought Michael. He would have to try to con him into that more often.

Carrying his pajamas, Michael stepped into the teeny bathroom, pulled the folding door closed, and turned to the sink.

If there had been room, he would have jumped back six feet. But there wasn't, so he jumped straight up and went "YEEEEEK!" when he saw the alligator in the sink.

Coming to the rescue, Dad stuck his head in, because that was all of him there was room for. Michael calmed down instantly. "Just a fake alligator alert," he explained. He threw the realistic-looking reptile out, aiming at Norman.

Norman ducked and laughed very hard.

After Michael took a shower, put on his pajamas, and brushed his teeth, he came out of the bathroom and checked his blankets to be sure Norman had not struck again.

Norman was eating crackers and clutching his fake alligator. Dad took it away and put it in the back bedroom. "No more alligator alerts tonight," he told Norman. "When you finish those crackers, be sure to brush your teeth again."

Dad went in the back bedroom with Mom. Norman brushed his teeth again. Since he had learned to get up into his bunk without a boost, he stomped across Michael's bed to get there. Michael aimed a halfhearted kick at him as he passed.

"Ha!" said Norman. "You missed!" He used the back of the driver's seat to climb up. There was a moment of quiet. Then with an earsplitting "YEEEEEK!" Norman flew straight out of his bunk and bounced on Michael's bed.

Under Norman's covers, where Michael had thoughtfully placed it, he'd found the fudge alligator.

Chapter 16

At Cypress Gardens they saw water-skiing and hang-gliding, and bird and alligator shows.

Walking in the gardens, through sunlight and shade, they saw trees and plants from all over the world.

"This is beautiful," Mom said, "everywhere you look."

Norman said, "I didn't know there are so many kinds of plants."

"They have eight thousand kinds here," Michael reminded everyone.

"You already told us that," said Dad. "Twice before we got here, and three times since we arrived."

Norman started to count plants to see if Michael might be wrong. Michael ignored him. He was sure he would fizzle out long before eight thousand.

Michael felt happy walking in the gardens, even though the chirping of birds was drowned out by Norman counting, "Twenty-three, twenty-four, twenty-five, twenty-six."

A voice behind them called, "Hey, Stanley, wait up!" Of course, his Stanley couldn't possibly be following him through Cypress Gardens, but Michael turned around anyway.

He thought someone was calling to a guy behind them named Stanley, but there was no guy behind them. There was Sarah, running ahead of her mother to catch up with Michael.

"Hi," she said. "We looked for your RV last night, but you weren't where I thought you were. My mom thought you'd left, but I said no. If you were going to leave, you would have said so."

Her mother caught up with them and introduced herself to Mom and Dad. "Hello, I'm Susan Sparks, the botanist Stanley must have told you about."

"Who?" said Dad, startled at the possibility Stanley might have said something.

"Dr. Susan Sparks. Not a medical doctor. I have a Ph.D. in botany. Didn't Stanley tell you about our conversation?"

Mom blurted out, "But that's not possible."

"But I really am a botanist," said Dr. Sparks, looking puzzled about their not believing her. She took a business card from her handbag and gave it to Mom.

Norman looked puzzled, too. "But Stanley never says anything," he blabbed. Mom silenced him with a look.

Dr. Sparks turned to Michael. "Didn't you tell them?" she asked.

"Of course he told us," said Dad.

Dr. Sparks looked even more baffled. "Let's start over," she said. "Yesterday, when my daughter and I met Stanley in the laundry room with his plant . . ."

Mom looked relieved. "His name is Michael."

Dr. Sparks turned to Sarah. "Why did you think his name was Stanley?"

"Some little kid waved at us and said, 'Hi, Stanley.' Why did you wave back if that isn't your name?"

"He was waving at my plant."

"You named your plant?" asked Dr. Sparks. "This is wonderful! I've always been fascinated with the close relationship some people have with their plants. They sort of treat them like pets, or friends, or members of the family. Is that how you feel about yours?"

"Sort of," replied Michael.

"You and your plant would be perfect for a study I've wanted to start for years." Dr. Sparks pulled a notebook and pen out of her handbag and started writing. "Why did you name it Stanley?"

"My brother started calling him—it—that. He thought it needed a name."

"Interesting that you think of it as a him." She made a note of that and turned to Norman, who looked as if he felt left out of all the attention. "Why did you think it needed a name?"

"My plant is my pet, and I named him Fluffy. So I thought Stanley should have a name, too."

Dr. Sparks looked up from her notebook. "What species is your specimen?"

"Huh?" asked Norman.

Sarah translated, "What kind of plant do you have?"

"The same as Stanley."

"Two of a rare species!" exclaimed Dr. Sparks. "This is exciting!"

Michael told Sarah, "You said you were coming here yesterday."

"We did," she replied. "We always spend two or three days here when we come to Florida."

"Because of the plants?"

89

"And the water-ski show. My whole family likes to water-ski."

"Where's the rest of them?"

"My father and my little brother go fishing while my mom and I look at plants. Next week we're going to the Everglades, so they can fish and we can study more plants."

"What's the Everglades?"

"A really big swamp in south Florida," she explained, "with fish and alligators and really great plants."

"My brother and I were in a swamp a couple of nights ago," boasted Michael.

Sarah looked impressed. "What kinds of plants did you see? Were there any alligators?"

"It was too dark to see," he replied.

"Gosh," said Sarah, "I've never been in a swamp when it was dark."

Norman bragged, "We got stuck in the muck."

Dr. Sparks was telling Mom and Dad, "Botany is endlessly fascinating. I really love my work!"

"I agree with you," said Dad, "about plants being interesting."

"Yes," Mom added, "sometimes positively amazing."

"Why don't we all get together for dinner tonight at our RV?" asked Dr. Sparks. "My husband's out fishing today, so we'll be grilling fresh fish, and we'll have plenty."

"I don't think we can," said Mom. "It's nice of you to invite us, and I'm sorry we can't come."

"That's too bad," said Dr. Sparks. "Maybe another night. I'd like to come over and take a closer look at your plants. Would tomorrow morning be convenient? Where's your campsite?"

"We just moved to a better one," said Mom, "and

we didn't memorize the number yet." That was true. They had moved in such a hurry, none of them could remember the number.

Dr. Sparks said, "No wonder we couldn't find you." She tore a page from her notebook and wrote on it. "Here's our campsite number. Please stop by and tell us where your RV is, or leave a note if we're not there."

Mom put the page in her purse without looking at it. They all waved good-bye as the two families went in opposite directions.

Norman started counting again. "Twenty-six, twenty-seven."

"You already said twenty-six before," Michael reminded him. "You should start with twenty-seven."

"Don't tell me what to do," said Norman.

After they left Cypress Gardens, they stopped at a nice restaurant for dinner and got back to the campground just after dark.

Dad looked in the rearview mirror. "Susan Sparks seems nice," he said. "I don't think she'd follow us to see where our RV is."

"I still think she might be after our plants." said Michael.

"Maybe she's a secret plant agent," Norman said.

"Don't be silly," Mom said. "She's found some unusual plants and just wants to learn more about them. That's natural for a scientist."

Dad said, "We can't hide out from these people for the rest of our vacation. We've got three more days, one to go to Sea World, and two just to relax before we start back."

"If they come after us," said Norman, "I can squirt them with my Water Blaster."

"No," said Mom.

"I can fill it up with syrup and get them all sticky so they'll be stuck to the ground and we can run away."

"No," said Mom.

"Then catsup," he suggested.

"No water blasting," Mom said, "with water or any other liquid. We'll just have to figure out how to handle their questions. You're right, we can't avoid them for three days."

"Good thinking," said Dad, slowing down to turn into their campsite. "Anybody got any ideas—besides syrup or catsup?"

As they parked, someone with a flashlight came around the side of the RV next to theirs. It was Sarah.

"My mom told me to ask you to come over," she said.

"You shouldn't be out in the dark by yourself far from home," said Mom.

"I just came out," said Sarah, "and I'm not far from home." She waved her flashlight at the lighted windows of the RV next door. The woman who looked up from washing dishes and waved back was Dr. Sparks.

Chapter 17

Mom walked over to the window. Dr. Sparks opened it. "Isn't this nice?" she said. "We're next-door neighbors, and we didn't even know it."

Mom said, "We can't come over tonight. How about having breakfast together tomorrow about eight o'clock?"

"We can each bring our own food so nobody has to do all the cooking," said Dr. Sparks. "We can use the picnic table."

"Great," Mom said.

Michael asked Sarah, "How did you find us?"

"I didn't really look at the RV that moved in here yesterday, and we were away quite a bit so I didn't see any people around it. Then tonight, when we were eating outside, I noticed it was the same kind as yours. When I couldn't find you before, some kids told me to look for the RV with the plants sticking out of the roof. This one had junk on the roof, so I climbed up the ladder to check, and there they were! Why did you move? Was there something wrong with the other campsite?''

''It's a long story,'' said Michael, ''and it's kind of hard to explain.''

''Sarah,'' called her mother, ''time to come in now.''

Michael went inside, too. He found Norman telling Mom and Dad, ''As soon as they go to sleep, we can move. Will they ever be surprised that we disappeared again!''

''No,'' said Dad. ''Pulling out would wake up everybody in the area, and there's no place to move to. We only got this spot because the office could give our old one to new people whom they were going to put here. The whole campground is full up.''

''We could start back home right now,'' said Michael.

''We could go to another shopping center,'' said Norman.

''We're not ending our vacation three days early,'' Dad said.

Michael asked Mom, ''Why are we having breakfast with them? We're trying to stay away from them.''

''We can't stay away. They're next door and being friendly. So we're stuck. We'll show them the plants after breakfast. There hasn't been any problem when people see them during the day.''

Michael protested, ''Everybody else who looked at them during the day wasn't a plant scientist!''

''Calm down,'' said Dad.

Norman looked upset. ''What's wrong?'' Mom asked.

''I don't want Dr. Sparks to get my plant,'' he wailed. ''She'll ask questions. She'll want to take him away and do experiments on him! Maybe Stanley, too.''

94

Mom gave him a big hug. "We won't let her take Fluffy. We have to keep him until Pet Plant Day. And in the morning I'm sure we can all think of good ways to handle any questions she thinks up."

Norman turned to his plant. "Think, Fluffy, think," he urged.

Michael started getting out socks to feed Stanley. "I got these mixed up," he said. "I'm not sure which are clean and which are dirty."

"That's easy," said Norman, holding his nose. "Just smell them. I can tell the difference all the way over here."

Norman selected an oatmeal and a chocolate chip sock for Fluffy's meal. They all got ready for bed and read for a while until they got sleepy.

After everyone settled in their beds, Norman climbed out of his and stomped across Michael's to get to the cupboard where his clean clothes were.

"What are you doing!" squawked Michael.

"I decided to wear my reindeer socks for breakfast. Maybe when I play 'Jingle Bells,' Dr. Sparks'll be so amazed she'll want to experiment on my sock instead of Fluffy."

He stomped back across Michael and put the socks on his pillow to be ready for morning.

Michael was almost asleep when Norman climbed down and stomped across him again.

"Now what!" he exclaimed.

"I'm filling my Blaster."

"Why?"

"So if Dr. Sparks sneaks in here tonight to swipe our plants I'll be ready to get her."

Michael thought this was so dumb that he did not bother to reply. He didn't ask whether Norman was filling the Blaster with water or syrup or catsup. He didn't care.

He was already asleep when Norman stomped back across him after filling it full of grape jelly.

As Norman was falling asleep, he pressed the sock with the musical microchip and hummed along. Since Fluffy liked singing, he was sure his plant was enjoying this, too.

In the middle of the night, after Fluffy ate the oatmeal and chocolate chip socks, he reached up into the bunk and picked up one of the reindeer socks. Then he reached over and put it back on the pillow. Apparently reindeer flavor did not appeal to him.

At breakfast they met Sarah's father and little brother, Max, who was a year younger than Norman. When Norman played "Jingle Bells," Max was fascinated. He wanted to try it, so Norman took off the sock and let Max put it on. Max walked around with his foot tinkling the tune three times. Then Norman put on his gorilla head, and the two of them walked down the road in time to the music to see if they could attract some attention.

Dr. Sparks looked at Mom and said, "Kids!"

Mom nodded sympathetically. "So true," she agreed.

"Can we go see your plants now?" asked Sarah.

Mom led the way and opened the door. Dr. Sparks stepped in, followed by everyone else except Max and Norman.

Dr. Sparks said, "If this is an unknown variation on a known species, this could be very important."

She looked Fluffy over very carefully and made some notes. Then she examined Stanley.

Norman and Max came back and squeezed into the

crowd. They had switched, and Norman had his sock back. Max was wearing the gorilla head. It was so crowded in the RV that Michael bumped his nose on somebody's elbow. "Stand back a little, please," said Dr. Sparks. Someone's foot pressed against Norman's sock and it began to play.

Mom told him to go outside until the tune ran out, but he didn't trust Dr. Sparks. He took the sock off and left it outside to play alone.

"Amazing," Dr. Sparks said. "The first time I saw Stanley I knew I'd never seen anything exactly like it before. Sarah, remind me to buy some film for my camera. I used it all yesterday at Cypress Gardens."

Sarah wrote that down in a little notebook.

"You're taking notes?" Michael said.

"I'm practicing to be a botanist," she replied.

Dr. Sparks said, "I've seen enough for now. Let's all go outside where there's more room and discuss this."

Uh-oh, thought Michael.

Norman was frowning.

"Now tell me," she said outside, "where did you get the seeds?"

Mom nodded at Michael. He explained about how he was always sending away for things, like offers on cereal boxes and coupons in magazines. It took so long for things to come, that when the Amazing Beans arrived in the mail, he could not remember what offer they were from. "Norman and I planted them," he said, "and they just grew."

"Very fast?" asked Dr. Sparks.

"Yes."

"Aha," she said and made a note. "Too bad there's no way to trace where they came from. But maybe other children who sent in for the same offer got the same kind of beans, too.''

"I never thought of that,'' said Michael.

Sarah said, "Then there could be more plants like this all over!''

"I want one like Norman's,'' said Max from inside the gorilla head.

"Take that thing off,'' said his father.

"After I take some pictures tomorrow,'' Dr. Sparks said, "I'll run over to Cypress Gardens and check with the botanists there and their reference materials to see if we can identify your plants. Now tell me anything you can think of that's unusual about them.''

Nobody answered her.

"Are they different in any way from other plants?'' she asked.

"We never had any other plants,'' said Norman.

"Mainly,'' said Michael, "they look weird.''

"I can see that,'' she said. "Anything else? And what do you feed them?''

"Feed?'' asked Michael. Could she possibly have guessed?

"What kind of plant food?'' she continued. "Liquid or powder? What brand? And how often?''

Michael was relieved. He could answer that.

"Just a bottle of green stuff I found under the sink. There wasn't any label. Then Mom bought some new stuff for us both to feed our plants. It was green liquid to mix in water.''

"I don't remember what brand,'' said Mom.

Michael added, "And I put little bits of food in the dirt around Stanley—broccoli, cookie crumbs, stuff like that. It was an experiment for our school science fair. That helped him grow faster than my brother's plant.''

"I didn't do that," said Norman. "My plant likes to be neat."

Dr. Sparks smiled as she wrote all this down.

Dad looked at his watch. "We really should get going soon if we're going to see everything at Sea World."

"We have to get going, too," said Mr. Sparks. "Now we won't take no about dinner tonight. We have plenty of fish left. How about six o'clock?"

"Fine," Dad said.

Chapter 18

At Sea World, the boys were so entranced with the leaping killer whales, the enormous sea lions, the penguins, and all the other wonders that they forgot about Dr. Sparks for a while.

Norman liked the penguins so much that he walked like one off and on all afternoon. People turned to look and smiled. Michael was glad he was not also wearing his gorilla head.

When they got back to the campground, Norman showed Max how to walk like a penguin, too. They waddled stiffly around the picnic table and down the road, laughing like crazy.

Sarah said to Michael, "Kids!"

"I know what you mean," he said.

After a great fish dinner, the two families sat outside talking until it got dark. Then the kids carried the dishes into the Sparkses' RV. Dr. Sparks washed, and Mom dried. Dad and Mr. Sparks cleaned up the outdoor grill and trash.

Michael could hear Dr. Sparks talking to Mom through an open window. "The boys don't seem to want me to study their plants. Every time I ask Michael a question, he looks as if he doesn't want to answer. Norman just scowls at me, as if I might do something awful to Fluffy."

"Yes," said Mom. "That's true."

Dr. Sparks continued, "I don't want to upset them, but I am going to check into what these plants might be."

Mom said, "We're leaving the day after tomorrow, so if you find out, be sure to write and let us know."

"I certainly will." Dr. Sparks wiped the suds off her hands and got her notebook. "What's your address?" She wrote it down. "If you ever need any advice on caring for the plants," she added, "I want you to call or write me anytime."

"I appreciate that, Susan," said Mom. "It's good to know help is available if we need it."

Michael sighed.

"What's the matter?" Sarah asked.

"I wish your mother wouldn't bother our plants. They don't like to be bothered."

"Why? She won't hurt them. She loves plants. And she might discover some new scientific knowledge."

Max asked Norman, "Can we play with your sock again tomorrow?"

"It has to get washed first," said Norman. "I never wear dirty socks. But I could put the microchip in a clean sock for tomorrow."

"Goody," said Max. He penguin-walked over to his RV and went inside.

When Norman put his reindeer socks in the dirty clothes basket, he took out the microchip and stuck it in one of a pair of fudge ripple. He put the clean socks in his bunk for the next morning and put out a chocolate chip and a cherry vanilla for Fluffy.

When he woke up, he reached for his sock to listen to "Jingle Bells" before he stomped across Michael to get to the bathroom. He pressed on it, but it was the wrong one. He felt around for the other one, but it wasn't there. He looked on the floor. Fluffy's meal was gone, and there was no other sock down there. Then he looked at Fluffy.

His plant looked very sick, sagging against the wall. Vines hung limply to the floor. Some leaves had fallen off. Others were slightly brown around the edges.

"Help!" yelled Norman. Nobody stirred. There was one sure way to get everybody up. He climbed into the driver's seat and sat on the horn.

Michael popped up like Dracula at sunset and said, "Huh?"

Dad hurtled out of the back bedroom, sidestepped Stanley in the kitchen area, fell over Michael's bed on top of Michael, and said, "Oof!"

Mom was right behind him, but ran smack into Stanley.

Now that Norman had everyone's attention, he wailed, "Something terrible happened to Fluffy!"

"He looks awful," said Dad.

"Sicker than Stanley did when he ate a plastic race car," Michael added.

Norman said frantically, "He ate a fudge ripple sock from my bunk."

"But he loves fudge ripple," said Mom.

"The 'Jingle Bells' microchip was in it," Norman explained.

"With the battery?" said Michael. "No wonder he's so sick."

As they stood there wondering what to do, Fluffy sagged a little lower against the wall.

Norman threw his arms around the plant. "Help, help!" he cried.

"I wish there were doctors for things like this," said Dad, helping him prop up Fluffy.

"There's one next door," Michael said. "Maybe we should call her."

"Hurry!" cried Norman with tears in his eyes.

Mom grabbed her robe and dashed out. She found Dr. Sparks and Sarah awake and putting on their robes to come over to see what the horn-blowing was all about. Mr. Sparks and Max had already left before dawn to spend the morning fishing.

"It's Fluffy," said Mom. "We need your help."

"What happened?" asked Dr. Sparks when she saw the suffering plant.

"You're a real plant doctor, aren't you?" Norman asked.

"Yes," she said.

So he told her that Fluffy ate the musical microchip and battery. She looked absolutely stunned at the news.

Sarah squealed, "It ate it? But how?"

"Be quiet," snapped her mother. "This is an emergency!" She carefully felt up and down the collapsing plant while Dad, Norman, Michael, and Sarah held it up.

Norman kept talking to Fluffy. "The plant doctor's here. She's going to make you get well."

Dr. Sparks kept pressing gently. When she got to a spot on a thick stalk not far from one of the ice-cream-cone–shaped leaves, she got results. Faintly, slowly, and very out-of-tune, "Jingle Bells" began playing.

103

"It's stuck right here," she said. "We'll have to cut it out before the battery acid poisons Fluffy any worse."

"OK," said Norman, looking brave.

"You can help me operate," said Dr. Sparks. "I need a clean paring knife."

Mom got her one.

"This is not going to hurt your plant," Dr. Sparks assured Norman. "I need you to hold this stalk while I cut."

"OK," he said.

It was over in a moment. Dr. Sparks sliced open the cut-off stalk and took out the chip and battery.

"How did this get inside Fluffy?" she asked.

Mom nodded at Norman to give him permission to tell.

"I told you. He ate it."

"Did you see Fluffy do that?"

"No, I was asleep."

"Then what makes you think he ate it?"

"It was inside his favorite flavor of sock."

"You believe your plant would eat a sock?"

"Yes," said Norman firmly.

"Where was this missing sock?"

"In my bunk."

Dr. Sparks pulled everything out of the bunk and searched through the sheets, blanket, and pillows. "Here it is," she said triumphantly, holding up a fudge ripple.

"No," Norman said, "that's the other sock, not the one with the microchip in it."

"The microchip must have fallen out, and the sock must be here somewhere," said Dr. Sparks.

"It's in Fluffy," said Norman.

From the expression on Dr. Sparks's face, Michael realized she did not believe this.

"Have you ever actually seen Fluffy eat a sock?" she asked.

"Yes," said Norman.

"When?"

"In the middle of the night when I woke up. That's the only time they do it."

"They?" asked Sarah. "Stanley, too?"

"Yep," Norman replied.

Dr. Sparks asked Michael, "Have you ever seen this happen?"

"Only if I wake up in the middle of the night," he said.

"How often do you do that?"

"Not very often," he said. "When I do, it seems like a weird dream."

"It does sound like a dream," said Dr. Sparks. But I'd better check this out. If by any chance the plants did eat socks, it would be a major scientific discovery."

Mom said, "Susan, you wouldn't tell anybody, would you?"

"Only if I could prove it," replied Dr. Sparks, "using scientific methods. First I would have to observe them eating socks—if they did—in their natural habitat."

"In your RV," explained Sarah.

Her mother continued, "That would have to be documented with photographs or videotapes. The next step would be controlled experiments to verify the behavior."

Norman looked alarmed at the word "experiments."

Sarah explained, "She means seeing if they do it in a laboratory under different conditions. With more pictures."

"I feel," said Dr. Sparks, "that this should be disproved so the boys won't go on believing any missing socks were eaten by their plants. Since you're leaving tomorrow, I'll have to do it tonight."

"While we're asleep?" said Michael.

"You won't even notice I'm here. You go to bed as usual. I'll wait in the dark to keep conditions as normal as possible. I won't turn lights on unless something happens."

"But first," she continued, "we have to take care of Fluffy." She sent Sarah to get some plant food from their RV. Dad and the boys carried Fluffy outside into the early morning sunlight and leaned him against the side of the RV. Sarah returned with a pail of water and tins of powdered chemicals.

"We mix our own plant foods," she explained, "for what different plants need."

While Dr. Sparks mixed food for Fluffy, Mom fixed breakfast for everyone. They hauled out the lawn chairs and ate with plates on their laps while they watched Fluffy.

After a while he definitely looked better.

Dr. Sparks said, "We'd better get Fluffy some clean soil. And both plants are getting too big for their pots. So we might as well repot them both while we're at it. There's a plant nursery not far from here. We can get what we need there."

Chapter 19

It took all of them to hoist the plants out of their old pots and into new, slightly bigger ones which would give the roots more room.

Dr. Sparks said she would take a nap so she could stay up all night.

"I have to stay up and watch her," said Norman. "Even though she saved Fluffy, I'm afraid she might swipe him."

"We'd both better take a nap," said Michael.

The family spent the rest of the morning at the swimming pool and had a cookout for lunch. It was peaceful sitting under the trees and doing nothing for a while. Mom and Dad went for a walk. Fluffy was standing strongly now, so the boys rolled him over to the playground.

"We're glad to see you," said Addie. "I was afraid you weren't coming over today."

Children gathered around. "Hi, Fuffy!" some said. "Where's Stanley?" called others. "What's the matter with Fuffy?" a little girl asked.

"Norman," said Addie, "did something happen to your plant?"

"He got sick last night, but he's getting better."

Addie suggested, "Maybe we can all help him feel better. We know he likes singing."

So Addie led everyone in singing "London Bridge," "Mary Had a Little Lamb," and "Jingle Bells." They had such a good time that even Michael joined in. Then they did the hokey-pokey. When they finished, Fluffy looked perked up, but the children looked pooped out.

"Nap time!" called Addie.

"We have to take a nap, too," Michael said. They headed back to the RV with Fluffy.

"I wish we could keep Dr. Sparks away from our plants," Norman said.

"We're stuck with her," said Michael.

Norman said, "Maybe she'll fall asleep before they eat."

"Not likely," said Michael. "But even though you told her what they do, she didn't believe it. So she's not really expecting them to eat socks. If we could only stop her somehow from seeing them do it, then maybe she'd leave them alone."

Norman thought very hard. Then he said, "Let's unhook the electricity. She can't see them eat in the dark."

Michael grinned. "Norman, I never thought I'd say this, but you just got a genius idea. I helped Dad with the connections when we switched campsites. I think I can unhook it by myself. If she tries to turn on the lights, by the time she figures out how to fix them, the plants will probably be through eating."

Norman warned, "Just don't do the wrong one and unhook the bathroom."

While they were lying down trying to take a nap, Michael was almost asleep when Norman said, "What if she brings a flashlight?"

That woke him up completely.

"Or a camera with a flash," added Norman. "Then what will we do?"

"We'll think of something," Michael replied. He lay there thinking as hard as he could, but he couldn't think of anything.

Norman said, "Maybe Fluffy won't feel good enough to eat tonight. Or maybe he had so much plant food he won't feel hungry."

"That would be nice," said Michael.

"But," continued Norman, "even if Fluffy doesn't feel like eating, she'll still see Stanley sucking up socks."

That gave Michael a glimmer of an idea. "Wait," he said. "What if both plants don't want to eat tonight?"

"I'm not doing anything that will make them sick," said Norman. "Not even for one night."

"Nothing like that," said Michael. "This is a great master plan that might actually work! Tonight we'll give them meals they don't like—dirty socks for Fluffy and clean ones for Stanley!"

Norman chuckled with delight.

They were ready when Dr. Sparks arrived carrying only her usual handbag. "I thought you boys would be asleep by now," she said, and sat down in the chair next to Fluffy. Michael noticed she was wearing soft slippers over her bare feet. He was glad she was not wearing socks. There could be trouble if Stanley was within reach of any socks that tasted like feet if he was really hungry.

109

Dr. Sparks said, "I'm just going to sit here in the dark and see if anything happens."

Mom said, "We've got to get a good night's sleep, but the boys took naps so they could keep you company."

"That's really nice of you," said Dr. Sparks. "I wish we could spend the night talking, but we're going to have to be absolutely quiet."

"Why?" Dad asked.

"So everything will be the same as any other night, as if everyone is asleep, so there will be nothing different to affect the plants' normal behavior."

"Well, then," Mom told Dad, "I guess we'd better just go in back and lie down."

Dr. Sparks turned out the lights in the main area. "Please turn off the lights back there, too," she asked Mom. "We need everything dark and quiet."

The lights in the back clicked off. Michael heard Dr. Sparks rummaging in her handbag. Then a little light went on in her hand. It was a pen with a tiny bulb on it. "This is for writing in the dark," she explained.

"Boys, would you please get in your usual places now? You can go ahead and go to sleep."

Michael headed for the door. "I left something outside," he said as he went out. He found his flashlight where he put it ahead of time and unhooked the electricity. Then he picked up a paperback book he had left outside on purpose, and went back in. Now Dr. Sparks could not turn the lights back on.

With just the pinpoint of light from the pen, Michael barely found his couch. He could hear Norman rustling around in his bunk. He got under the covers of his couch bed and tried to relax.

"I don't think I can sleep," he said.

"Then just close your eyes," said Dr. Sparks, "so you'll look asleep."

Nobody said anything for a long time. Could Norman have gone to sleep that fast? Or was he faking? Michael watched the light from Dr. Sparks's pen move back and forth across her notebook. He wondered what she was writing.

"Waiting is really boring," he said.

"I'm used to it," she replied. "I can't tell you how many times I've stayed up late with plants that bloom only at night."

"Really?" he said. "I never heard of anything like that before!"

"It's fascinating," she said. "I'll tell you all about it later. Right now we have to maintain silence."

He shut up and watched the little light. Then he saw her put the pen down and open her handbag. She took out a tiny tape recorder, a flashlight, and a small flash camera and put them on the table next to her.

Michael hoped his master plan would work. Then maybe her lights wouldn't matter.

In spite of his determination to stay awake, he drifted into sleep. Now the only sounds were even breathing from Michael, Norman, and the back bedroom.

Chapter 20

What woke Michael was the flash and whirring noise of the camera. He saw Dr. Sparks's flashlight propped up to cast light on what Stanley was doing. One of his vines was lifting a sock! Oh, no, thought Michael, he's so hungry, he doesn't care that it's clean!

But when Stanley raised the sock to his ice-cream-cone–shaped leaf, he paused. Then he dropped it. Dr. Sparks was taking pictures as fast as she could—flash, whirr, flash, whirr. Stanley picked up the second sock in front of him and did the same thing. Then his vine groped around, searching. Finding no dirty socks, the plant stood still. Dr. Sparks kept aiming the camera, waiting for Stanley to make another move. Nothing happened.

The plan was working so far. Now it was up to Fluffy.

Soon, behind Dr. Sparks's back, Fluffy started to move. While Michael held his breath, the plant picked up each of the two dirty socks in front of him and did the same thing. There would be no *schlurrp*, no burp, and no ''Ex'' from Fluffy tonight.

What happened next startled Michael so much that he almost said "No!" out loud. Fluffy picked up one of the dirty socks again, and tried to throw it in Stanley's direction. But he was still weak, and the sock did not go far. It hit Dr. Sparks in the back and fell on the floor.

She turned with her camera, but not fast enough. She got a picture of Fluffy doing nothing.

She kept turning back and forth, aiming at one plant and then the other. But nothing more happened. After a while she sat back down and wrote very fast in her notebook.

Michael closed his eyes and fell asleep.

Dr. Sparks woke him when the sun was coming up. "These plants are amazing!" she said excitedly. "They didn't eat socks, of course, but Stanley picked them up with a vine and dropped them. I got that on film. And while my back was turned, the socks in front of Fluffy were moved. One of them hit me in the back. I didn't see it, but my theory is that he picked it up and threw it!"

"Amazing," said Michael, trying to look surprised. "Just what you thought I dreamed when I woke up in the middle of the night."

"Apparently it wasn't all a dream," said Dr. Sparks. "The plants moved so quietly that I didn't get anything on the tape recorder except camera noises and me swearing when I stubbed my toe on Fluffy's skateboard wheel. But I did get a whole roll of pictures."

Michael saw she was rubbing her foot.

"I'll get some ice for your toe," he offered.

"Thank you," she said. "Do you realize what this means?"

"Your toe hurts?"

113

"No, the plants' behavior. This is a great discovery! And think of the possibilities! A plant that can pick something up and drop it could be developed to pick up litter, like in parks, and throw it into trash cans!"

"Wouldn't it get tired?" asked Michael.

The ice trays were full of water. Leaving the refrigerator door open, he carefully carried one for her to put her foot in. "The ice melted," he said, "but this is sort of cool."

"These plants could be wheeled around on skateboards to wherever there is trash! This could be a major breakthrough for cleaning up the environment," said Dr. Sparks, plopping her foot into the tray. The water slopped over the edges.

"Perhaps some could be developed to sort trash for recycling," she went on. "Or to pick up junk around the house. Parents with messy kids would love . . . oh, no!"

Michael turned to see what she was looking at. Stanley's vine was creeping toward Dr. Sparks's camera on the kitchen counter. It was quite a bit bigger than Dad's radio.

Michael froze. But Stanley passed by the camera, grabbed the roll of film sitting next to it, and whisked it into the refrigerator. Michael heard a little splash.

As this was happening, Dr. Sparks jumped up. The tray on her foot started sliding sideways toward Fluffy. She grabbed Fluffy to keep from falling, swung around, stubbed the toes on her other foot, and swore.

All this awakened Norman. He groggily saw the dreaded botanist clutching his plant as if to swipe it, appearing to kick the skateboard, and saying words his mother would not let him use.

Grabbing his Blaster, he flew out of his bunk to the

114

rescue. He bounced twice on Michael's bed with blood-curdling karate yells, and let Dr. Sparks have it with a heartfelt squirt of grape jelly.

He quickly realized, however, that jelly does not squirt as far as water or syrup. Much of it oozed downward onto his bare feet and Michael's bed.

But that didn't stop Norman in defense of his beloved Fluffy. He sprang to the floor on gooey purple toes and let Dr. Sparks have it again, this time at close enough range to glop up her sweatshirt at the waist. That was as high as the jelly would ooze.

She started swatting him on the head with her notebook.

Awakened by Norman's horrifying karate noises, Mom burst out of the back bedroom like a mother bear in defense of her cub. "What are you doing to my child?" she yelled.

"What is he doing to me?" yelled Dr. Sparks. "I thought my Max was the strangest kid in the world, but yours takes the prize!"

Norman protested, "She was swiping my Fluffy! Or attacking him! Maybe both!"

"He attacked me first!" exclaimed Dr. Sparks. "With purple sticky goo! What is this stuff?"

"Grape jelly," said Norman. He smiled winningly at her to try to weasel out of what he had done. To show her that it was not harmful, he aimed the Blaster downward and squirted some more on his toes. "It feels good," he said.

They all burst out laughing.

"Just promise me," Dr. Sparks said, pointing at the Blaster, "cross your heart and hope to die, that you won't tell Max you've got one of those."

Norman promised.

Dad came out of the back bedroom. "What's going on?" he asked.

"You're not going to believe it," said Michael.

Mom asked Dr. Sparks, "Why do you have an ice tray on your foot?" The two women started laughing again so hard they could barely talk.

Michael slipped out to hook up the electricity. When he came back in, Dr. Sparks and Mom and Norman were explaining to Dad in between fits of giggles.

They were getting calmed down by the time Dr. Sparks told them about her plan to clean up the world with plants.

At that Dad burst out laughing.

"I'm serious!" she said.

"That would take a lot of plants," he said.

Dr. Sparks stood up and asked Mom, "What's the best way to get all this grape jelly out of my shirt?"

"Try Maxi-Clean detergent," advised Mom. "If it doesn't come out, you can smear some peanut butter on it and put it between two pieces of bread." The two women burst out laughing again. Michael thought they were definitely going goofy.

When they finally got themselves under control, Dr. Sparks gathered up her things and asked Michael to find where Stanley had dropped her film.

He stepped to the refrigerator and fished it out of the orange juice pitcher. He put it on a plate to catch the drips and handed it to her.

"Oh, dear," said Mom. She got some paper towels.

"My pictures!" exclaimed Dr. Sparks. "They're probably ruined!" She looked really upset.

"Maybe," said Michael, "Stanley did it because he didn't like the camera noise or didn't want his picture taken."

"You have a wonderful imagination," replied Dr. Sparks. "You should write stories." She turned to Mom and Dad. "Would you be willing to sell me one of the plants so I can continue my research? If it's all right with the boys, of course."

"No," said Dad. "Unfortunately, we promised they could keep them until their school's Pet Plant Day in the fall."

"What do you mean by 'unfortunately'?" she asked.

"They're more trouble than the usual plants," remarked Mom.

Dr. Sparks looked so tired and disappointed that Michael felt sorry for her.

"But plants that pick up and drop things I'm sure have never been discovered before," she said. "A scientist has to pursue something like this. Would you mind if I took some cuttings?"

"That would be all right," said Mom. "Wouldn't it, boys?" They nodded.

Michael whispered to Mom. She said, "We have to have a family conference, Susan. We'll be right back."

They went outside. Michael suggested they give Dr. Sparks some seeds. Mom and Dad agreed. "We can mail her some as soon as we get home," said Dad.

"Maybe we don't have to wait until then," said Michael.

Back in the RV he said, "Stand back," and opened his clothes cupboard. A snarl of clean and dirty clothes and assorted junk fell out. He dug into the pile left inside. Squashed at the bottom he found the pants he had worn the day they left home. In a pocket were the pods he had picked off Fluffy when he first put the plastic cover over him.

117

"Authentic Fluffy pods," he announced and handed them to Dr. Sparks.

"Once in a while," said Mom, smiling, "your talent for messiness comes in really handy."

"This is wonderful!" exclaimed Dr. Sparks. "I'll plant them right away! What can I do to thank you?"

"Just keep us posted on your research," said Mom. "And if you discover that the plants really do eat socks at night, see if you can train them to eat something a lot cheaper."

Dr. Sparks laughed hilariously at what she thought was Mom's big joke.

Michael whispered to Norman, "She still doesn't believe us, but she'll find out."

Chapter 21

The two families had breakfast together before packing up to leave.

Sarah and Max were very excited about the news of the plants' ability to pick up and drop things.

"I'm going to take notes every day while the seeds are growing," said Sarah. "And I'll send you some pictures when they get big."

"Your notes are going to be really interesting," said Michael.

"What do you mean?" she asked.

"You'll see," he replied mysteriously.

Dr. Sparks told Michael about the night-blooming plants she had worked with.

"That's amazing," he said.

"I'll send you a good book about it," she said. "And another interesting book about plants for Norman."

"Gee, thanks," said Michael.

Dr. Sparks put some more film in her camera and told the kids to line up for a group picture. They scrunched together and smiled. But when she looked through the lens, what she saw was Max wearing Norman's gorilla head, Michael holding two fingers in a V behind Sarah's head, Sarah crossing her eyes and sticking out her tongue, and Norman aiming his Blaster at Michael's head. She took the picture anyway.

Michael said to Norman, "Get that thing away from me! I don't want jelly in my ear!"

"It's empty," said Norman.

Max's eyes lit up. "Where do you get one of those?"

"Oops," said Norman to Dr. Sparks. "I forgot."

"I want one," said Max.

"No," said his mother.

Max asked Norman, "You squirt jelly with it?"

"Not anymore," he replied. "I ran out."

Max looked very disappointed. Norman whispered to him. Max looked surprised and then started to smile. "Only clean ones?" he whispered back. Norman nodded. Max looked delighted.

Max and Norman penguin-walked down the road one more time. Then it was time to leave.

The Sparks family pulled out first. Everyone waved until they were out of sight.

Michael climbed to the roof to put the plastic coverings over the plants' tops and tuck them into the vents.

Before leaving the campground, they drove past the playground, honking and waving good-bye to Addie and the children. "Good-bye, Fuffy! Good-bye, Stanley!" the children called. Norman picked up one of Fluffy's vines and waved it at them through a window.

Once on the highway the boys fell asleep because they had stayed up so late the night before. Later they had to do some of the homework they had neglected for most of their vacation. "I'd rather count trucks," grumbled Michael.

Norman insisted on counting trucks and doing his

homework at the same time, but Dad made him be quiet.

The whole trip home was fairly peaceful. The plants behaved, eating just their socks. Dad taped the refrigerator door shut at night, just in case.

On the last morning of the trip, when Norman woke up early, he had trouble untaping the refrigerator door. So he sliced the tip off the tail of the fudge alligator. He thought Grandma would not mind. It tasted so good, he sliced off another piece.

Pretty soon, though, he realized that candy for breakfast wasn't a good idea. His stomach didn't feel good, so he went back to bed.

Late that afternoon, they turned down their own street and into their own driveway at last. Bob appeared as they were unloading the RV. Norman couldn't wait to tell his vacation news.

"I went on Space Mountain five times," he said.

"Wow!" said Bob.

Norman added casually, "I ate alligator meat."

"No kidding!" Bob said, looking very impressed.

"And," Norman bragged, "I got stuck in a swamp at night in the dark!"

"Are you ever lucky!" exclaimed Bob. Norman went on and on, entertaining him with his vacation adventures.

Michael called Jason to tell him about the vacation, but there was no answer.

When he carried in the gift box for Grandma, he thought how good a little piece of fudge would taste—just a very little piece from the tip of the tail, where it would be hardly noticed.

He opened the box. The fudge alligator had no tail at all! Only one person would have sliced it off so neatly.

Michael broke off a paw and ate it. Delicious! He ate another paw.

"Hey, Bob," he called. "Want to taste some alligator? It's good. Norman loves it. I'll get you both a big piece."

Bob and Norman bounded into the kitchen. "Sure," said Bob.

"Where did you get alligator?" asked Norman suspiciously.

Michael gave Bob a fudge paw before Norman could see what he handed him. Bob turned to Norman as he chewed.

"This tastes great!" he said. "Have some."

Norman looked a little green.

Bob swallowed and smiled. "Can I have another piece?" he asked.

Norman looked a little greener.

"I didn't know," Bob said, "that alligator tastes just like fudge."

"It doesn't," said Norman. "Aha!" he exclaimed. "Grandma's alligator!"

Bob looked puzzled. "Your grandma cooked this alligator?" he asked. "How did she get it in the pan?"

"It's not real," explained Norman. "He's playing a joke. It's fudge made to look like an alligator." He went around Michael and found the box. "You ate three paws!" he said.

"You ate the tail first," replied Michael.

"Mom's going to be mad," said Norman.

"That's not my fault. You started it."

In came Mom with an armful of kitchen things. She saw the open box. "Who did this?" she demanded.

"Michael," said Norman.

"Norman started it," said Michael.

"It's wrecked," said Mom. She broke off the last paw and ate it. "Mmmmm, this is good," she said. "Now what am I going to send my mom for a Florida present?"

"A postcard?" said Norman.

"You could still send it to her," suggested Michael. "If we cut the head off, it wouldn't look like a wrecked alligator. It'd look like just a big bunch of fudge. It'd still taste good."

"We could eat the head," said Norman.

"I can help," said Bob.

"Later, after dinner," Mom said. "You've had enough for now. Too much candy is not good for you."

Dad came in with another pile of stuff. "This is the last load," he said. "We're ready to get the plants out."

The boys went to help him, while Mom sat down at the kitchen phone to call Grandma to let her know they were home.

As they rolled Stanley and Fluffy in, Mom said, "She's not home. I left a message on her answering machine to call us when she gets back."

Dad said, "As long as we're going out to return the RV, we might as well eat dinner out."

They invited Bob to go along and called his mother to tell her.

"We can put everything away later," said Dad. "We have to get the RV back by six."

Off they went, leaving Stanley and Fluffy standing by the door to the kitchen.

Chapter 22

The house was dark when they got home after having dinner, doing some shopping, and dropping Bob off.

Turning on a living room lamp, Mom asked, "Who wants some fudge for dessert?"

"Me," said everyone.

Outside the kitchen door, she stopped and said, "Didn't you leave Stanley here?"

Michael ran after her. Next to the kitchen door Fluffy stood alone.

He went in the kitchen and turned on the lights. Stanley stood next to the refrigerator. Michael was glad to see the door was closed.

Then he noticed the cord that ran from the refrigerator to the phone. He opened the door. Sitting on a shelf was the receiver, saying, "What's going on? Michael? Norman? Is that you kidding around? Say something! Are you all right? Should I call your local police?"

He picked up the receiver. "Grandma?" he said. "Is that you?"

"Of course it's me! Who else would let the phone ring for five minutes because I thought you might be out in the RV? Who else would be worried to death because when the phone was finally answered there were funny noises and nobody said anything? Are you all right? What happened? I heard rustling noises, and then a door slammed."

Michael sighed. How could he explain that his plant answered the phone, probably because he was irritated by the long ringing, and then left her to talk to the inside of the refrigerator?

"I'm sorry, Grandma," he said, "it wasn't my fault. And don't worry. We're all OK."

"What on earth is going on there?" demanded Grandma.

Michael handed the phone to Mom. "It's for you," he said.

Dad remarked, "I'm glad there wasn't any orange juice in there. At least we don't have to buy a new phone."

Norman suggested, "Let's get an answering machine like Grandma's, so Stanley doesn't have to answer the phone anymore."

Mom was telling Grandma, "Somehow Michael's plant knocked the phone off the hook, and it wound up in the refrigerator. Mother, stop giggling! I'm not kidding!"

She put her hand over the phone. "My mother," she said, "is having a laughing fit."

"Dr. Sparks didn't believe us either," Norman pointed out.

After Grandma stopped laughing, Mom told her about the trip and that she was sending her some fudge that looked funny but tasted good. Then Grandma wanted to speak to Michael.

"You know that piece of your plant I broke off to try to identify it? I used some rooting powder on it. It sprouted roots, and I planted it in a flower pot. I think it grew two inches last night."

Michael asked, "Is it getting vines yet?"

"Very little ones are just starting. I put the plant on the side of my bathroom sink. It's a warm, sunny spot, good for growing."

Michael did not recall that Grandma left any dirty socks lying around in her bathroom, so maybe there wouldn't be a problem.

After Michael hung up, Dad asked, "How do you suppose Stanley got in the kitchen? I'm sure we left him out there with Fluffy."

"In Florida one day," Michael said, "I thought I saw him leaning back and forth at the playground to try to get his skateboard rolling. But I'm not sure."

"Does the floor slant downward a little here?" asked Dad. "Could he have just accidentally rolled in?"

"I don't think so," said Michael. The boys rolled the plants back to their room, where they would be away from opportunities for trouble.

At bedtime Michael was hungry. In the refrigerator he found that Mom had mixed a pitcher of orange juice. He drank some and poured a little glass to take to Stanley.

He sprinkled some juice on the inside of his plant's ice-cream-cone–shaped leaves and poured the rest around the roots.

As he snuggled down under the covers, he thought he heard a low hum that sounded like "Mmmmm."

In the morning Michael was eager to get to school

and tell everybody about his vacation. Chad was the first friend he ran into in the hall.

"I went on Space Mountain five times and ate alligator and went in a swamp in the dark," Michael told him. "Anything interesting happen here while I was away?"

"Everybody's excited about their new plants," said Chad. "Mine is just starting to grow. It won't be long before it's almost as big as yours."

"What kind is it?" asked Michael.

Chad looked puzzled. "The same as yours. Didn't Jason tell you?"

Michael's stomach felt like the first plunge down Space Mountain.

"Where did you get it?" he asked.

"Jason sold me a seed."

Michael was furious. He knew Jason was a little sneaky once in a while, but he didn't think he would act like a real rat.

Chad said, "I thought he got them from you."

"He did," said Michael, "only I didn't know it."

"He stole them?" asked Chad.

"Not exactly. He got me to promise him seeds if the plants ever got any. So he must have helped himself and didn't tell me."

"What are you going to do?" asked Chad.

"I don't know," replied Michael.

Then he noticed Jason at the far end of the crowded hall. He ducked into the boys' bathroom to avoid him. He waited until the last minute to go to their classroom so he wouldn't have to talk to him.

At recess, Jason was very busy talking to other guys. He was avoiding Michael.

Talking to others, Michael found out six more class-mates had bought seeds. No one said anything about socks, so apparently Jason had not told them. They were all excited about bringing their new plants to Pet Plant Day in the fall. "They won't be as big as yours," said one kid, "but the principal and the custodian will really be surprised."

As the class went back inside, he got pushed near Jason in the crowd. Michael felt so angry that he didn't want to speak to him.

But Jason suddenly spoke to him. "How was your vacation?"

"Fine," said Michael, walking away.

Jason came after him. "I didn't swipe the seeds," he said. "You promised me some."

Michael was still furious, but all he said was, "How many did you take?"

"Just a couple handfuls."

Michael tried to picture how many pods would have fitted into Jason's pockets. Then he got up his nerve.

He said, "You better give me back the ones that are left."

"I sold them all," said Jason, "and I need some more for the waiting list. I'll ride over after school."

Michael glared at him.

"What are you looking at me like that for?" asked Jason. "I was going to give you half the money." He walked away, leaving Michael feeling like a fool for not standing up to him.

Norman came to find Michael at lunch. "Did you hear what Jason did?"

"I heard."

"We gotta get him for this," said Norman.

"He's coming over after school," said Michael. "We'll have to have a master plan ready by then."

"I'll fill up my Blaster," Norman said, grinning. "Syrup this time. Jelly doesn't squirt far enough."

Michael got an idea that was worth a try. "Orange juice," he told Norman.

"Why?"

"I'll explain later."

Chapter 23

Mom was not home because it was one of her after-noons to work. The boys hurried to get ready. Norman filled his Blaster. In their room Michael pulled the shades down and closed the curtains to make it as dark as possible for the plants. He put a chair between the beds with its back to the plants. Norman went to get Bob, who agreed to help. Michael got out his little radio, tuned it to a heavy metal station, and turned it off. He brought in the phone from Mom and Dad's room. The cord was long enough to stretch across the hall.

Bob waited as lookout at the living room window. After a while, he yelled, "Here he comes!"

"Watch for the hand signal in the window," Michael reminded him. Bob hurried out the back door, as Nor-man opened the front door. "My brother's in with the plants," he told Jason.

"Oh, hi," said Michael casually. He was sitting on his bed holding his little radio, which he had just turned on very loud. Norman quickly sat down on his own bed, so the only place left for Jason was the chair.

"I brought some of the money," said Jason, handing it to Michael. "I'll bring you the rest of your half later. I need thirty-six more seeds for the waiting list. You might as well make it an even fifty."

"Hold this a minute," said Michael, handing him the radio. "No, don't turn it off. That's Stanley's favorite station."

"He has a favorite station?"

"Stanley learned to do some new stuff on vacation."

"Like what?"

"Did you tell the kids you sold the seeds to that these plants eat socks?"

"No. You made me promise not to. It doesn't matter. Nobody would believe it anyway."

"What are you going to do if they find out?"

"They'll be surprised. Who cares? It'll be too late to ask for their money back."

Michael made a little hand signal at Norman, who reached behind the curtains and shade and waved to Bob.

"Want to see what Stanley learned?" asked Michael. "No, don't turn around. Sit still."

Jason stayed put with the little radio in his hand still blasting.

Michael picked up some of Stanley's vines and wrapped them around Jason and the chair.

"Neat trick," said Jason, "but you did that, not Stanley."

Norman pulled his Blaster from the bedside table drawer. "Want to see my Water Blaster?" he asked.

"I already saw it," replied Jason.

"I bet you don't know what's in it," said Norman, waving it around wildly.

"Be careful with that thing," warned Jason.

"Oops," said Norman, squirting orange juice all over Jason's hair.

"Stop that!" squawked Jason angrily. He tried to get out of the chair. "I can't move!" he exclaimed. "Get this plant off me!"

"Maybe my finger slipped," said Norman. "See? Like this!" He squirted a little more.

"What is that stuff?" yelled Jason.

Michael was trying not to laugh out loud.

"Do something!" demanded Jason.

One of Stanley's vines plucked the radio from his hand and threw it against the wall. It stopped blaring. A couple of Stanley's other vines started gathering orange juice drops from Jason's dripping hair and chin. The rest of the vines stayed snugly wrapped around Jason and the chair.

"This plant is an octopus!" shouted Jason. "It tickles! Get it off me!"

"No more seeds," said Michael.

"But I've got a waiting list!"

"Give the money back."

"No."

The phone began to ring.

"Aren't you going to answer it?" asked Jason.

"No," said Michael. It rang on and on.

"Are you going to get this plant off me?"

"As soon as you promise to give back the money to the kids on the waiting list. And tell everybody you sold seeds to that they're growing sock-eaters."

"They'd think I was lying," responded Jason. "They'd laugh at me."

"And give them their money back any time, now or later, if they want it."

"Answer the phone," said Jason. "It's driving me crazy!"

One of Stanley's vines picked up the receiver and threw it, but the coiled cord bounced it back onto Jason's lap. He shouted at it, "Hello? Help! I'm being held prisoner at a yellow house on Elm Street!" He paused to listen for an answer. What he heard was Bob, laughing like crazy.

"OK," said Jason, "I'll do what you want. I shouldn't have taken the seeds without telling you."

While Michael unwrapped him, Fluffy picked up the empty Blaster and bonked Jason on the head with it.

"Fluffy's helping," said Norman proudly.

As Mom and Dad pulled in the drive, they saw Jason speeding away on his bike.

"What was Jason doing here?" asked Dad. "I don't like him being here when your mother or I aren't home."

"He looked wet," said Mom. "Were you guys messing around outside with the hose?"

"It's a long story," said Michael.

"Then you'd better start right now," said Dad.

"You might not like this," Michael continued, stalling.

"We'll see," said Mom. She opened the refrigerator. "What happened to the orange juice? It's almost all gone."

"We didn't drink it," said Norman helpfully.

"Then where is it?"

Michael took a deep breath and began. "It's all over Jason," he explained. He told them what Jason had done and how he came over to get more seeds.

"We decided to sic Stanley on him," Norman said.

"Norman blasted him with the orange juice," said Michael, "because Stanley is attracted to orange juice."

"Fluffy helped," boasted Norman.

"And Jason's going to stop selling seeds and give the kids their money back if they want it."

Mom asked, "You made this orange juice mess in your room? And you're both going to clean it up? Every sticky little drop?"

"It's not too bad," said Norman. "I put the plastic from the RV all over to keep the rug clean."

"We'll wipe the walls right away," said Michael. "It won't be easy, but it was worth it!"

"Considering what Jason did," said Dad, "somehow I can't get too upset about this."

"Me either," said Mom, trying not to smile. Then she added sternly, "But don't ever do it again."

"What is going to happen when Jason tells the kids he sold seeds to that they're growing sock-eaters? Some of them may not want their money back."

"Things are getting out of control," said Mom. "We started with two plants that were enough trouble by themselves. Now we have a botanist and her children growing some, kids at your school growing some, and my own mother! I hope Susan's research will find how to stop them all from eating socks."

"First, she has to find out that they do," said Michael. "But that won't take long."

Chapter 24

After dinner the boys worked on cleaning and home-work. Mom decided they should all go to bed early because they were tired from the first day back at school and work.

When he was ready for bed, Michael went to get a little orange juice for Stanley. He ran into Mom in the hall.

"Are you hungry?" she asked.

"No, this is for Stanley. I poured a little on him last night, and he seemed to like it."

"Not tonight," she said. "Put it back. We need what little is left for breakfast. I'll buy plenty more tomor-row, so then we'll have enough for Stanley, too. Maybe we can get him to like that better than socks."

"If we get both plants to do that," asked Michael, "can we keep them after Pet Plant Day?"

"Maybe," replied Mom, "especially if they turn out to be scientifically valuable."

As Michael was falling asleep, he was thinking about the seeds sprouting in different places. He wondered what Grandma might name her plant.

Norman murmured sleepily, "We have to tell Grandma pretty soon about the socks."

"Maybe my orange juice experiment will work," said Michael. "I think I'll start taking notes tomorrow."

"You're turning into a botperson," mumbled Norman.

Then there was silence. Norman sounded like he was asleep.

Michael whispered, "Good night, Stanley. We're a great team." As he drifted off, Stanley put a vine on his pillow and patted his head.

At Chad's and Jason's and thirty-six other kids' homes around town, new little plants were peeking up, about two inches high.

Somewhere near the Everglades six seeds in six pots were sending little shoots out, still under the dirt, in the Sparks family's RV.

There were also tiny plants sprouting unnoticed where Fluffy had shed pods at both their Florida campsites, outside Addie's house and in the swamp.

In Grandma's bathroom, her plant's tiny vines were trying to pick up a washcloth.

As Michael and Norman snoozed peacefully, Stanley reached out a vine to grab the bedpost at the end of Michael's bed. He pulled himself over to it. Then he reached for the doorknob and rolled right out the door into the hall. There, he felt around and found enough doorknobs and furniture to grab to keeping moving. Down the hall he went, heading for the refrigerator and humming "Mmmmm."

It wasn't long before Fluffy followed.

EXTRA! EXTRA!
Read All About It in...

THE
TREEHOUSE
TIMES

(#8) THE GREAT RIP-OFF
75902-0 ($2.95 US/$3.50 Can)

(#7) RATS! 75901-2 ($2.95 US/$3.50 Can)

(#6) THE PRESS MESS
75900-4 ($2.95 US/$3.50 Can)

(#5) DAPHNE TAKES CHARGE
75899-7 ($2.95 US/$3.50 Can)

(#4) FIRST COURSE: TROUBLE
75783-4 ($2.50 US/$2.95 Can)

(#3) SPAGHETTI BREATH
75782-6 ($2.50 US/$2.95 Can)

(#2) THE KICKBALL CRISIS
75781-8 ($2.50 US/$2.95 Can)

(#1) UNDER 12 NOT ALLOWED
75780-X ($2.50 US/$2.95 Can)

MEET THE GIRLS FROM CABIN SIX IN

CAMP SUNNYSIDE FRIENDS SPECIAL:

CHRISTMAS REUNION   76270-6 ($2.95 US/$3.50 Can)

(#9) THE NEW-AND-IMPROVED SARAH
                       76180-7 ($2.95 US/$3.50 Can)
(#8) TOO MANY COUNSELORS   75913-6 ($2.95 US/$3.50 Can)
(#7) A WITCH IN CABIN SIX   75912-8 ($2.95 US/$3.50 Can)
(#6) KATIE STEALS THE SHOW   75910-1 ($2.95 US/$3.50 Can)
(#5) LOOKING FOR TROUBLE   75909-8 ($2.50 US/$2.95 Can)
(#4) NEW GIRL IN CABIN SIX   75703-6 ($2.95 US/$3.50 Can)
(#3) COLOR WAR!   75702-8 ($2.50 US/$2.95 Can)
(#2) CABIN SIX PLAYS CUPID   75701-X ($2.50 US/$2.95 Can)
(#1) NO BOYS ALLOWED!   75700-1 ($2.50 US/$2.95 Can)
MY CAMP MEMORY BOOK   76081-9 ($5.95 US/$7.95 Can)